THE
REVENGE OF THE
INVISIBLE
GIANT

THE DUNDOODLE MYSTERIES

THE REVENGE OF THE INVISIBLE GIANT

DAVID O'CONNELL

ILLUSTRATED BY
CLAIRE POWELL

BLOOMSBURY
CHILDREN'S BOOKS
LONDON OXFORD NEW YORK NEW DELHI SYDNEY

For my sister Helen

BLOOMSBURY CHILDREN'S BOOKS
Bloomsbury Publishing Plc
50 Bedford Square, London WC1B 3DP, UK

BLOOMSBURY, BLOOMSBURY CHILDREN'S BOOKS and the
Diana logo are trademarks of Bloomsbury Publishing Plc

First published in Great Britain in 2020 by Bloomsbury Publishing Plc

A catalogue record for this book is available from the British Library

ISBN: PB: 978-1-5266-0746-1; eBook: 978-1-5266-0747-8

2 4 6 8 10 9 7 5 3 1

Printed and bound in Great Britain by CPI Group (UK) Ltd,
Croydon CR0 4YY

To find out more about our authors and books visit www.bloomsbury.com
and sign up for our newsletters

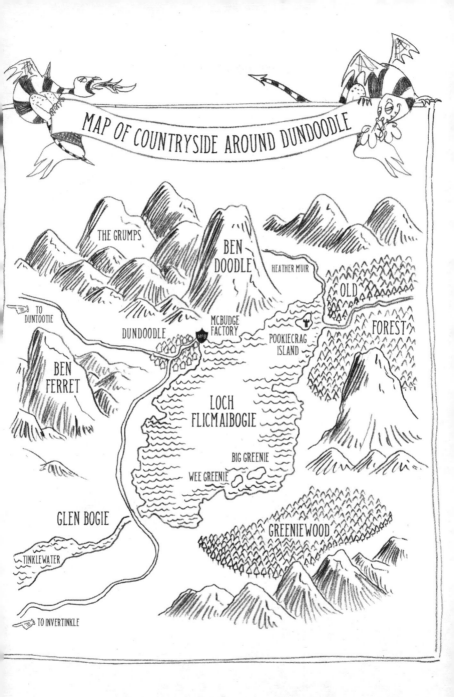

Sherbet the dog was snoring. He'd found a soft patch of moss growing at the edge of the forest clearing and had settled down for a snooze. Fluffy, skittish squirrels, plump, loping rabbits and that bad-tempered, one-eyed cat called Bogbrush that lived over at Fraser's Fishmongers – Sherbet merrily chased them all through the fields of his dreams.

Something tickled him on the nose. He opened one eye. In front of his face, a seedling sprouted out of the ground, its stem increasing in size at an alarming rate, leaves unfurling rapidly. The dog jumped to his feet and watched as the plant continued to grow at Jack-and-the-Beanstalk-like speed.

'Mind out, Sherbet!' called Archie, as the dog gave a bark of fright. Archie's hands were pointing at the plant, now a sturdy sapling, and his forehead was creased in concentration. He wiggled his fingers as if he was moulding the tree out of the air.

Sherbet gave a sigh. His master was messing around with magic again!

Grow, thought Archie. *Grow fast, grow strong.* He could feel the magic flowing through the ground beneath his feet and channelling into the plant, urged on by his willpower and the gestures he'd been taught. Three odd little men stood around Archie, following his movements intently, as more and more leaves emerged from the newly formed branches. The sapling snaked upwards, joining the surrounding forest in its fresh spring attire.

'Keep your focus, Archie,' encouraged one of the men. 'It's working.'

His eyes fixed on the tree, Archie directed more magical power into its sap. *Grow, grow, grow.*

SET ME FREE …

It wasn't so much a voice as an echo, but Archie heard it clearly, carried by the breeze from across the loch. Old, craggy and angry, the words sent a shiver down his spine.

'Who said that?' Distracted from his task, Archie's hands relaxed, causing a branch to curl round and round like a pig's tail before poking one of the little men on the nose. The tree's unnatural growth stopped abruptly.

'Who said *what?*' replied the man, rubbing his nose testily. 'Pay attention to what you're doing, boy! You're trying to make the tree grow, not turn it into a hat stand.'

Archie looked at the three of them, puzzled.

'Didn't you hear it? A voice. It sounded like it came from … far away.' He waved vaguely towards the mountains.

'We heard nothing, Archie McBudge,' said the little man. His cloak, made from woven leaves, rustled in irritation, and a robin that was nesting in the hood directed a dismissive chirrup at Archie.

The man and his two brothers were, in fact, brownies – the Fjurge Brownies: Jøkchip, Jøknut and Dubbeljøk. They were just some of the magical folk whom Archie had met since he had come to the strange little town of Dundoodle over a year ago. Gnomes, mobgoblins, tree spirits and honey dragons – they were as much part of Dundoodle's wildlife as the pine martens, mountain hares and golden eagles that haunted the mountains and forests, and, like them, they kept out of the way of most humans.

Archie was now one of those magical folk himself, since he had inherited the powers gifted to the McBudge family. But he was still learning how to use those powers and become a *wyrdworker*. It was hard, but the Fjurge Brownies were helping him. They couldn't do wyrdwork themselves but had watched generations of McBudges in action, so they knew what was needed.

'Right, let's score Archie's performance on this task,' said Jøkchip, ignoring the mystified look on Archie's face. The brownies each held up a broad leaf with a number on it.

'Seven,' declared Jøkchip. 'A good effort but a few rough edges. Room for improvement.'

'Eight!' said Dubbeljøk. 'You totally owned it, Archie. I liked the flourish at the end.'

'Four,' said Jøknut.

'Only four out of ten?' said Dubbeljøk, giving his brother a sharp look.

'He lacks artistic flair,' said Jøknut with a defensive sniff. 'And I'm sure I saw some illegal pinkie-finger waggling going on.'

'I think we've probably done enough wyrdwork training for today,' said Dubbeljøk, with a sigh, eyeing Archie's preoccupied face. 'The boy's obviously tired. Why don't you come and have a cup of tea with us, Archie?'

'I'm not tired …' Archie began.

He was sure he hadn't imagined that strange voice. But he'd never been invited for tea with the brothers before, so he shrugged off the incident and followed the brownies through the old forest, Sherbet trotting by his side. Jøkchip's robin, named Brunhilda, led the way, darting from tree branch to tree branch ahead of them.

'You're doing well,' Jøknut reassured him, as they scrambled through a newly grown clump of fern. 'That clearing will soon be filled with young trees, now that you've learned the *Coaxing of Seedlings* spell. The damage caused by the Mirk will soon be undone.'

Archie shivered at the mention of the evil spirit that had caused so much destruction the previous summer. Thankfully, he and his friends had defeated the monster before it had destroyed one tree in particular: the majestic Wyrdie Tree, which was the source of all magic in Dundoodle.

Archie couldn't help but smile as they approached it. He was always impressed by the sight of the Tree, towering over the rest of the forest. It was also where the three Fjurge brothers lived. They tended to its everyday needs whilst Archie was learning to be its magical Guardian, a role that had always been held by a McBudge.

'I feel like I should be doing more – learning faster,' he said. 'Is there a *Coaxing of Rainfall* spell too? That would help get things growing.'

'There's no need for that in these parts,' chuckled Jøknut. 'You need to have patience, Archie. Learning takes time. Anyway, your magic is earth magic, drawn up from the roots of the Tree. You've no jurisdiction over the other elements of fire, air – or water.'

'The only magic we perform with water is making a nice cup of tea,' said Dubbeljøk contentedly. A squirrel that had been hiding in the folds of his cloak leaped on to a branch and scampered up into the Wyrdie Tree's branches. 'Ratatoskr is leading the way. He wants his tea too!'

Using notches in the Tree's massive trunk, Dubbeljøk pulled himself up into the canopy, where the brownies' home lay hidden. Archie, carrying Sherbet, struggled to keep up with the nimble little man as he disappeared through the layers of leaves. They were surrounded by green in all its different shades, so that even the light that played around them was a rich emerald. Archie felt safe under this vast protective roof and could understand why the brownies had built their house here.

Looking up, he saw how the meandering branches had

woven
themselves
around each other
and the main trunk,
forming what looked like
a giant bird's nest from the
outside, a higgledy-piggledy knot of
wood perched high above the ground.
Tiny windows inserted into gaps reflected
the jewelled light, and a crooked chimney
poked out from its top to leak a lazy stream
of smoke towards the sky.

Dubbeljøk's feet disappeared
through a leaf-covered hatch in
the structure and Archie followed,
just able to squeeze himself
through the brownie-sized hole.
Inside he found a tidy but cosy
little sitting room. Bookshelves and
storage cupboards were fashioned
from alcoves in the trunk, benches
and tables from curved boughs. The
floor was covered in moss, ferns and
woven leaf mats. Niches in branches

hid small lamps or candles. The whole room could have grown directly out of the Tree. Archie couldn't tell if it had been made by magic or the brothers' skill, but either way, he loved it.

Whilst the brownies busied themselves with the tea things, Archie peered from a window, curious to see the view from such a great height. The loch was a mirror of the pale grey of the morning sky. Misty Ben Doodle rose above it, the last of its winter snow slowly retreating to form a white cap on top of the mountain. The breeze felt fresh against his face.

'I can taste salt in the air,' he said.

'Aye, the west wind comes from the ocean,' said Jøknut, placing tea bowls on the table. 'The spring storms blow sea spray right over the mountains.'

Archie stared into the direction of the breeze, searching the horizon for a glimpse of the sea. But suddenly there was the strange voice cutting through his thoughts again, a harsh whisper. And despite the warmth of the brownies' sitting room, its words sent a chill through his heart and made the hairs on the back of his neck stand up.

SET ME FREE … SO I CAN BRING DESTRUCTION TO THE WORLD.

Archie glanced back at the brownies. They were bickering over whether to use the best or second-best sugar bowl for their guest. They'd obviously not heard anything. How was that possible? Jøknut beckoned him to the table.

'Tea's ready,' the little man said. 'And we've still some of the ginger cake from that gnome of yours.'

'That gnome' was Tablet, the McBudge family's ancient butler, who was actually *half*-gnome. The brownies disapproved of gnomes for some reason, but Tablet's baking was slowly winning them over.

Archie sat down at the little table and helped himself to some cake. He decided to keep quiet about the voice until he worked out what was going on.

Meanwhile, the brownies were reminiscing.

'We've not seen the sea for hundreds and hundreds of years,' said Jøkchip, feeding some worms to Ingeborg the mole, who normally slept in his sleeve but was now snuggled into a cushion on the table.

'And if I ever see it again it will be hundreds and hundreds of years too soon,' spluttered Dubbeljøk. 'I've never been so sick in all my life as when the troll ship brought us here from the north. The sea roared and rolled like a dragon with bellyache!'

'Was that when you brought the Wyrdie Tree seedling with you?' said Archie. He'd never heard the full story of how the Tree had arrived in the forest near Dundoodle.

'It was a terrible night of storm, chaos and disaster!' Jøknut said merrily. He slurped from his tea bowl, then cleared his throat with relish. 'The World Tree, which linked the realm of the old gods to that of men, was in danger!

'The gods were under attack from the giants, who were sent by a band of evil warlocks. The warlocks wanted to control mankind without the gods' interference, to make humans their slaves. They commanded the giants to uproot the enormous World Tree and break the mystic link, severing the connection between the gods and their mortal human children. In return, the warlocks promised to give the giants eternal life.

'The gods defended the Tree and only just fought off the giants. They couldn't be sure they'd win again. So, in case the worst should happen, Compostabelle, the goddess of nature, grew a seedling from the Tree. She charged us, the Fjurge Brownies, to find a safe place to grow it, so that link would endure, if the Tree should fall.'

'The Viking trolls brought you here in their ship,' said Archie, who knew this bit, 'and the seedling became the Wyrdie Tree …'

'A dreadful voyage!' said Jøknut, as his brothers nodded with the grim memory. 'We were chased by an angry stone giant, who strode across the ocean in pursuit of the troll ship. We thought we'd be crushed by his flinty fist or dragged down into the dark, churning water, never to be seen again. The ship filled with our cries of terror …'

'When it wasn't filled with the sound of us chucking our guts up,' put in Dubbeljøk. Ratatoskr giggled.

Jøknut glared at his brother for spoiling the moment. 'Brownies are not seafaring folk,' he admitted.

'But the sea is on the other side of the mountains from Dundoodle,' said Archie. 'How did you get here?'

'The god of the sea, Maldemer, came to our aid,'

Jøknut replied, back in storytelling mode. 'He gave the troll captain a magic key that opened a tunnel from the sea, through the mountains to the loch, and our ship escaped into it. The giant must not have been able to fit into the tunnel, because he never caught us.'

'But the tunnel was strange and dark,' said Jøkchip, taking up the tale, 'and we cowered in the ship, afraid of what it might hide.'

'The vessel rocked and spun in its uncanny currents,' continued Dubbeljøk, 'hurling us from one side to the other. And then – *disaster*! We lost *The Book of the Earth*!'

'*The Book of the Earth*?' said Archie, who was already sitting on the edge of his seat because of its size, but edged a little further forward anyway.

'*The Book of the Earth* – containing all the forest traditions and wyrdie-knowledge of generations of brownies – vanished overboard in a chest that came loose in the commotion.'

The brothers looked mournful.

'There is so much more we could teach you if we had *The Book of the Earth*,' sniffed Jøkchip, wiping a tear away. 'Spells of root and sap and twig! The lore of the plant spirits! The songs of the woodland streams! The secret of the Anyfruit vine!'

'The Anyfruit vine?' said Archie.

'A vine whose fruit could be any food you desired, and always delicious! We have only those spells that we managed to remember. Oh, the magic that was in that book!'

'It was a marvel we didn't lose the seedling overboard,' Dubbeljøk pointed out. 'That would have been a real disaster.'

'And *we* made it through,' finished Jøknut. 'We lost the Book but we had been saved! The Wyrdie Tree was brought to the forest, where it grew in secret until the gods finally won the war.'

'Why didn't you go back for the Book?' said Archie. It sounded like such a powerful object. He wouldn't need to bother with all these lessons if he had *The Book of the Earth* – he'd be a fully fledged wyrdworker in no time.

'The brave Viking troll captain, Prang the Pebble-dashed, used the key's magic to close both entrances of the tunnel forever, in case the giant should find its way through and discover the whereabouts of the young Wyrdie Tree. Then he hid the key. The trolls bade us farewell and walked into the mountains, carrying their ship on their mighty shoulders as they began their long journey home.'

'It was only then that we realised the Book was missing,' said Jøknut.

'Speaking of going home,' said Archie, finishing the last bit of cake, 'I need to be getting back across the loch or I'll be late for Tablet's Sunday dinner.' He picked up Sherbet and was about to clamber through the hatch when Jøknut handed him a package. It was a box wrapped in leaves and tied with a vine.

'This is for you,' said Jøkchip. 'It is fragile and will need looking after carefully.'

'What is it?' asked Archie, holding the box gently.

'Inside is a seedling for you to keep,' said the brownie. 'A young Spirit Oak. We give one to each Guardian, and we think you're ready, Archie.'

'Is it magic?'

'It's no Anyfruit vine, if that's what you're thinking. The oak will grow into whatever form you choose. Some might let it grow straight and make a wand or staff, like that of a wizard, or the handle for a broom, like a witch.'

'Or you can make it curly like a hat stand,' added Jøknut, grinning. 'The tree will sense your need, but it is up to you what kind of charmed instrument you finally create.'

'Thank you,' said Archie sincerely. This gift sounded powerful. He hung the box from his shoulder and slowly made his way back to the ground, Sherbet nervously dangling from under his arm.

The two of them hurried through the trees to the shore of the loch, where Archie's enchanted boat waited. As it ploughed across the water, heading for the concealed cavern underneath Honeystone Hall, Archie wondered if the boat might have been made by the Viking trolls.

'It definitely wasn't made by the brownies,' he chuckled, running his hand along the vessel's smooth prow as it was buffeted by the strengthening breeze. 'They'd have no use for it themselves. And it certainly looks Viking-ish, with the dragon's head on the end.'

Thoughts of dragons made him glance at Pookiecrag Island, whose ruined castle hid the entrance to the lair of his friends the honey dragons. They would be coming out of hibernation soon. It would be wonderful to see them again. Did they remember the arrival of the troll ship, so many years ago?

Back at the Hall, Archie and Sherbet took the secret

passage that led from the cavern to the ancient house's library. Giving a nod to the painting of Great-Uncle Archibald – whose ghost occasionally made an appearance when Archie needed help – Archie carried the leaf-covered box down the hallway to the vast greenhouse attached to the back of the building. The Hall had its own private jungle, thanks to all the overgrown plants that grew there. Archie thought this might be the best place for the Spirit Oak.

'It's still a bit frosty outside,' he said to Sherbet, as he unwrapped the box. 'And the wind can be brutal. The seedling will be safe and warm here.'

The box contained a clay pot, filled with rich, dark earth. A pair of delicate green leaves grew from a dainty stem, newly emerged from the soil. Archie picked up the pot to look more closely at the magical plant, holding it up to the grimy window. A dark shape momentarily blocked out the light – there was someone outside, watching him!

Sherbet barked and sprang to the window, knocking Archie's elbow and sending the pot flying from his hands.

Archie could only watch in horror as it hit the tiles with a sickening CRASH!

The pot shattered, releasing an explosion of soil that flung the fragile plant into the air. It landed roughly, on top of a heap of dirt and broken pottery.

'Sherbet!' cried Archie, as the dog hid under a banana plant, with his tail between his legs. 'What have you done?' He wanted to go and find out who had been watching him, but he couldn't leave the precious Spirit Oak like this.

'Don't worry! We're here to rescue you once again, Archie McBudge!'

It was his friends Fliss Fairbairn and Billy Macabre (also known as MacCrabbie), both smiling broadly as they wove their way through the foliage. They had come for dinner – Tablet made the best roast potatoes anyone had ever tasted, and nobody refused an invitation to eat at Honeystone Hall.

Archie heard a buzzing sound at his ear and turned to see a honey dragon hovering at his shoulder and eyeing the broken pot curiously. It was Blossom, who lived in the greenhouse during the winter, as she didn't like to hibernate with the rest of the dragons. Fliss had been teaching her to speak and they'd grown fond of each other.

'Someone's made a mess!' squeaked the little creature, settling on Fliss's head.

'Hello, Blossom!' said Fliss. 'Now the Dundoodle Detectives are all present and correct!'

'Was that you outside the window?' Archie asked them. 'It gave me quite a scare.'

'No – your mum let us in the front door,' said Billy, raising an eyebrow. 'We didn't see anyone outside. Hang on! Is that … is that a Spirit Oak?' The boy ran to the pile of earth and stared with wide eyes at the forlorn seedling. 'It's a magical plant! The Spirit Oak has a rating of five out of ten on my Creepy Scale.'

'It'll be a dead magical plant if you don't get it into the ground,' said Fliss. She gently scooped up the seedling and, using a piece of broken pot as a spade, quickly made a hole in one of the large flower beds and dropped the Spirit Oak into it. 'Give it a watering regularly and it'll be fine,' she said, patting the soil around it firmly.

'Or you could use a bit of wyrdworking to help it on its way,' said Billy, with a sly grin. He was an expert on all the magic in Dundoodle, and was fascinated by Archie's role as Guardian of the Wyrdie Tree.

Of course, thought Archie. *The Coaxing of Seedlings spell!* He wiggled his fingers and concentrated.

The others watched as the drooping plant recovered itself, its pale leaves getting greener by the second. What could he have learned if *The Book of the Earth* hadn't been lost? An Anyfruit vine – it sounded amazing!

'Not too much,' said Archie, relaxing his hands and letting the magic ebb. 'I haven't decided what I want it to grow into yet.' He explained to the others about the Fjurge Brownies' gift.

'I hope you're not thinking of making anything too complicated,' said Billy, uncertainly. 'It looks a little wonky.'

'If we don't stop talking and go to dinner soon,' said Fliss, 'it'll never grow into anything – as I'll have to eat it! Come on, I'm famished!'

They left Blossom in the greenhouse (she only ate nectar, from flowers that grew there) and followed the smell of cooking to the kitchen.

Having never located the dining room amongst Honeystone Hall's maze of corridors, Archie and his mother ate all their meals in Tablet's cosy domain. The children found the butler and Mum dishing up dinner in a fog of delicious aromas.

'Good afternoon, Master Archie,' the old gnome wheezed. 'And Miss Fairbairn and Master Macabre too. Excellent. There's plenty of food for everyone.'

The lights flickered as Tablet's dangerously shaky hands ladled gravy on to the plates, sending peas skittering in all directions. Sherbet made a grab for any escapee vegetables that made it as far as the floor.

'The electricity is very erratic today,' said Mum.

'It usually is at this time of year,' said Fliss. 'The power cables go over the mountains and sometimes the pylons get blown down in the spring storms. They've been talking about sorting it out for years.'

Archie half listened as he helped himself to potatoes, his mind elsewhere. He wanted to tell the others about the mysterious voice he had heard in the forest, but as Mum knew nothing about his magical escapades – or that there was a dragon living in their greenhouse and a ghost in their library – he decided it would have to wait. He still hadn't worked out who had been watching him either. It couldn't have been Mum or Tablet, as they had been busy in the kitchen.

He put the thought to one side as they discussed the school trip that was taking place the next day.

'Where is it you're going again?' asked Mum, as they tucked into their dinner. 'I'm afraid I still don't really know the area around Dundoodle very well.'

'The seaside,' Archie answered, without any enthusiasm. 'We're taking a bus to some freezing cold place on the other side of the mountains to go and look at seaweed.'

'We're going to study the rock pools for our science

class,' Fliss said, throwing him a scornful glance. 'I think it will be fascinating. I love finding out about nature and the environment. Don't you, Billy?'

But Billy looked glum.

'I would if it didn't mean having to spend the day with my mum,' he sighed. 'She can be *so* embarrassing.'

'Your mum?' said Archie. He didn't know much about the MacCrabbie family, as Billy liked to cultivate an aura of mystery about himself. He always wore black and stayed away from bright sunlight, which wasn't difficult in Dundoodle.

'Dr Yasmeen MacCrabbie,' explained Fliss. 'She's an environmental scientist who works at the Marine Research Centre we're going to visit. I think it's brilliant that your mum's an important scientist, Billy.'

'She's such a *geek*,' he said. 'She can talk about mud worms and sea slugs and ecosystems for hours.'

'And that's coming from Lord Geek of Nerd Castle in the land of Dorkington!' said Fliss. 'Well, I'm looking forward to our trip anyway. I can't wait to visit Trollhaven...'

The lights flickered again, as if auditioning for a bad horror film.

'*Trollhaven?*' Archie almost spat out his carrots.

'Archie, don't talk and eat at the same time,' said Mum. Fliss and Billy exchanged a look. The place name obviously meant something to Archie.

'There are lots of legends about it,' Billy said, perking up. 'Ships that have disappeared inexplicably. Giant sea creatures. Enchanted whirlpools ... Creepy Scale rating of seven point eight.'

Fliss gave Archie a knowing smile.

'It sounds like just your kind of thing,' she said.

It wasn't until the next day that Archie had a chance to speak to the others alone. They were on the school bus, which was filled with their excitable classmates and stressed-out teachers, driving to Trollhaven.

The road to the sea took a winding route through the mountains known as the Grumps. Mr Fingle, their teacher, was attempting to explain some of the highlights of the landscape.

'On the right, you can see a fine example of an igneous extrusion, heavily glaciated,' he said, over the general chatter.

'That's a rock,' said Fliss.

'And on the left, a collection of ancient gneiss, overlaid with metamorphic quartzite …'

'More rocks,' groaned Fliss, fidgeting in her seat.

'And up there, Gorm's Bones – a group of granite megaliths used thousands of years ago to create a stone circle ...'

'Rocks, rock, rocks!' said Fliss, as Mr Fingle's waffle merged into the inattentive chatter. 'When are we going to get there?'

She leaned over to Billy and Archie, who were in the seats next to hers.

'And why did you choke on your veggies when Trollhaven was mentioned yesterday, Archie? Do I smell an adventure?'

Archie grinned and passed her a bag of McBudge Fudge. He had inherited the McBudge Chocolate Factory from his great-uncle, along with Honeystone Hall. Archie called being the owner of the factory his 'third job', after being a schoolboy and Guardian of the Wyrdie Tree, but he took them all seriously, and worked on inventing new sweets when he had the chance.

'No adventures,' he said. 'It was just a funny coincidence.'

He told them the tale of the troll ship, the giant and *The Book of the Earth*.

'I'd bet anything that the giant chased the ship across

the sea to Trollhaven. That would explain how it got its name. The tunnel to the loch must have its entrance there.'

'It would fit with the legend of the ship disappearing,' agreed Billy, nodding. 'It did disappear – into the mountains!'

'Something else unusual happened yesterday,' said Archie. He told them about the voice he'd heard.

Fliss frowned. 'Have you got bats in the McBudge belfry?' she said. 'That's completely bonkers!'

'I knew you wouldn't believe me!' Archie said. 'But I didn't imagine it – honest.'

Fliss shrugged. 'Then why didn't the brownies hear it?' she said.

Billy rubbed his chin thoughtfully.

'Your great-uncle said that you could sense magic,' he said. 'If this voice were magical in some way, then maybe only you could hear it. Perhaps it was a message to you. Or perhaps you were eavesdropping on a conversation of some kind.'

'You're a magical satellite dish,' scoffed Fliss. 'We'll be able to use you to tune into Radio Hogwarts!'

Archie ignored her. 'I really hope it wasn't a message, because it didn't sound like it was coming from anyone I'd want to meet.'

The small fishing village of Trollhaven seemed grey and unwelcoming as the bus parked on the seafront. Huddles of squat houses sulked on the cliffs overlooking the bay as the cold wind swept in from the sea. In contrast, the Marine Research Centre was a bright, new building next to the harbour and Billy's mum was there to greet them, much to his mortification.

'Welcome, all!' sang out Dr MacCrabbie, as they clambered off the bus. 'And a special hello to my little boy. I'm glad you put your thick coat on, William – I wouldn't want you to get chilly.' There were giggles from some of the other children.

'You haven't got some kind of invisibility spell amongst your collection, have you?' Billy whispered to Archie, looking as if he wanted the ground to swallow him up.

'Sorry, *William*,' Archie replied. 'Embarrassing parents are immune to my magic.'

'We're going to have a tour of the Centre, so you can see the marine conservation work we do here,' announced Dr MacCrabbie. 'Then we'll visit the beach so you can study the biodiversity within the rock pools for yourselves.'

Despite Archie's misgivings, the visit turned out to

be rather interesting. Billy's mum was passionate and knowledgeable, much like Billy himself, and able to answer Fliss's many detailed questions. It was not long before they were on the beach, pottering around in the seawater pools left behind by the tide, seeking the small fish, crabs and shrimps that inhabited them. The children were split into groups, with Archie, Billy and Fliss sent to explore the shoreline near the cliffs.

'I wonder if we'll see any sign of the tunnel,' he said to the others, as they scrambled over the seaweed-covered rocks. The cliffs were sharp and jagged, with hidden coves and salt-scarred inlets. It was the perfect place to conceal a ship, or a secret cave, but there was no sign of any tunnel entrance. Archie sighed in frustration.

'What did you expect?' said Fliss. 'A great big troll-sized keyhole, surrounded by piles of brownie sick?'

'Of course not!' said Archie, quickly pushing that exact thought from his mind.

'And look – there are some workmen over there.' Fliss pointed to a group of men who seemed to be digging at the base of the cliff. 'I think they'd have noticed a ship-sized door.'

'It was a long time ago,' Billy said. 'The Wyrdie Tree's been growing in the forest since way before the McBudges were around. The sea will have washed away any signs of the tunnel, if the tunnel is actually here. We're only guessing about the name.'

The children put their minds to their schoolwork, recording the sea creatures they'd found in the rock pools. After an hour or so, Dr MacCrabbie blew a whistle to get the children's attention.

'The tide will start coming in soon,' she called across the beach. 'Everyone needs to head back to the Centre.'

Archie gave one last look at the cliff face then reluctantly turned to follow the others. As he jumped from rock to rock along the beach, he noticed a small group of women silently watching the children from the harbour wall. Why were they so interested in the school party? At that moment, a powerful sound flooded into his head, so powerful the shock of its impact knocked him sideways. It was the voice – but so much louder than before.

Fliss saw him wincing in pain. 'Archie, what's the matter?' she said.

He didn't answer, he couldn't hear anything other than the voice. Its words were lost in the echoing, shuddering vibration in his head, but he recognised the anger and the terrible desire, and it filled him with fear. Staggering, struggling to stay upright, Archie's boot slipped on the damp seaweed underfoot and he tumbled over, narrowly missing a sharp rock.

He lay on the ground, stunned. The sound gradually began to fade, but for a long moment Archie couldn't move. As his head cleared, the words began to form, to focus.

SOON. SOON I WILL BE FREE. FREE TO DESTROY…

There was a shout – it was Fliss – and then another, deeper voice. A man, frowning with concern, knelt over Archie. He wore a hard hat and a fluorescent jacket. Dr MacCrabbie stood behind the man, breathless and worried.

'Are you all right, lad?' the stranger said. 'You took a bit of a fall there. Lucky not to hit your noggin.'

Archie pulled himself up on to his elbows. His head was still reeling.

'I think he slipped,' Fliss said feebly. She knew there was more to it.

'And I thought *I* had a dangerous job!' The man laughed through his beard and, with a pair of burly arms, swung Archie up on to his feet. His workmates looked on

mutely from the cliff.

'It was so lucky you and your colleagues were around, Gilbert,' said Dr MacCrabbie.

'Yes, thank you,' said Archie, feeling slightly foolish. 'I'm fine.'

Fliss changed the subject.

'Why's your job dangerous?' she asked the man eagerly. 'Are you some kind of engineer? I want to be one too.'

'That's right,' said Gilbert. He reached into his jacket

and presented Fliss with a business card. 'Gilbert Thaw's the name. Tunnelling's my speciality. You have to be very careful of rockfalls, landslides and the like. We're taking some rock samples from the cliffs around Trollhaven.'

The children glanced at each other.

'Tunnelling?' said Archie.

'Mr Thaw and his friends work for a company that wants to lay a power cable to Dundoodle from the wind turbines out at sea,' explained Dr MacCrabbie, pointing at the giant white windmills that dotted the distant horizon. 'It'll replace the pylons and overhead wires that get blown down in the spring storms.'

'Finally!' said Fliss. 'No more spooky flickering lights and TVs switching themselves off. Dundoodle can come out of the Stone Age.'

'The shortest way is to blast a tunnel in a straight line *through* the mountains,' said Gilbert, grinning. 'The alternative is to dig a trench *over* the mountain. But that would take much longer and be much more expensive. We need to work out which route is best, and the good doctor here is helping us.'

'How, Mum?' asked Billy, as if the idea of his mother helping anyone was unfathomable.

'I'm working as the environmental consultant,' she

said. 'Both options could have an impact on the local wildlife and it's my job to make sure there's as little disturbance to nature as possible.'

'Hopefully, we'll find a way to please everyone,' said Gilbert, going back to his work with a friendly wave.

'We'll see,' whispered Dr MacCrabbie. 'I think there'll be quite a bit of opposition to either blasting or digging. There have already been complaints from an environmental group. If only there were some other way.'

She ushered the children back to the Centre. Archie noticed the group of women who had been watching them had vanished.

As the bus took them back to Dundoodle, Archie told the others about the voice. His face was so pale from the shock that Fliss didn't doubt him this time.

'You must have been really close to … whatever it was, for it to be so loud,' she said.

'I'll do some research amongst the old books in your library,' said Billy. 'Maybe I can find some clues there on spirit voices.'

'It's odd,' said Archie. 'I didn't sense any magical presence, like I did with the Mirk. It's like it's close but distant at the same time.'

Fliss shivered at the mention of the Mirk. Archie

remembered how it had controlled her with its magical spells. It had left her wary of magic for a while afterwards.

'Let's hope it stays far away,' she said. 'One evil spirit was quite enough.'

When Archie got home from school, Mum told him that Fliss's dad, who was manager of the chocolate factory, had asked for a meeting with him.

'Mr Fairbairn wants to talk with you about some of your ideas,' said Mum carefully. 'I'm not sure they've all been entirely … successful.'

Puzzled, Archie took the passage that linked the Hall to the factory next door, and found Mr Fairbairn in his office. He greeted Archie warmly, but he looked a little sheepish.

'Mr McBudge,' he said, offering Archie a chair. 'We've been testing some of your designs for new sweets. The Fizzfires you invented last year were very popular, but I'm afraid your latest batch of inventions haven't worked quite so well. But fear not, it's early days in your career as a confectioner and there are bound to be some setbacks.'

'What kind of setbacks?' asked Archie. He didn't like the sound of this. Mr Fairbairn cleared his throat nervously.

'The Long-Lasting Liquorice Bootlaces ...' he began.

'Yes, they're much better than the ordinary ones. You can chew and chew and chew—'

'And chew and chew and chew. In fact, they're almost completely indestructible. Miss Fozzle in Research has had to stop speaking for a week to let her jaw recover, though that's not without its benefits. We could use them as actual bootlaces, but I'm afraid as sweets they're inedible.'

'Oh well ...' said Archie, getting up to leave.

'And then there's the bubblegum ...'

Archie sat down again.

'The Inflatabubble Gum? I thought the idea of gigantic bubbles was a good one!'

'Oh definitely, Mr McBudge! But Mr McDiddle – you know how short of stature he is – he got trapped inside one of the bubbles and it was so rubbery that it took several people to get him out. He was like a hamster running around in one of those plastic balls! Now, imagine if that happened to someone's granny or pet dog?'

Archie pictured Sherbet floating away in a huge pink bubble.

'OK – back to the drawing board with that one as well,' he said. 'Now, I'd better be going ...'

'And about the Jelly Teddies,' continued Mr Fairbairn, a smile fixed on his face.

'You don't like them either.'

'I don't think chips-and-curry-sauce flavour is going to be a huge seller. Especially after our trial tastings. Unless we sell them with a bottle of mouthwash.'

'Anything else?'

'The Extra Extra Extra Extra Strong Mints – possible fire hazard. Thankfully our test laboratory has sprinklers installed.'

Archie sighed.

'I guess I need to work on my ideas,' he said. *But what if I had* The Book of the Earth? *he thought. I could conjure an Anyfruit vine to grow any sweet I wanted. There'd be no need for testing!*

'Don't be downhearted, Mr McBudge,' said Mr Fairbairn, cheerily handing him a bag of sweets with the label REJECTS stuck on it. 'It just takes practice, and trial and error. Sometimes you need to have bad ideas to be able to learn to recognise a good one.'

Archie couldn't face bringing his rejected sweets back to the Hall, but he also couldn't face throwing away all his hard work, so he decided to store the bag in Fliss's hideout, a treehouse-like den secreted up in the pipework of the factory's roof. The children would often use it as a meeting place, as it was hidden away from prying eyes and ears.

Climbing into the hideout, Archie was surprised to find Billy sitting at its rickety little table. He had a writing book open and was busily scribbling some notes into it. He'd helped himself to Fliss's 'secret' stash of McBudge Fudge, and offered Archie the bag as he came in.

'I just wanted to update my *Book of Wyrdiness* with your tale of the troll ship,' he said between chews. 'The power is off in our street, so I came here.' As the factory had an electricity generator, it wasn't affected by Dundoodle's power-supply problems. 'If only we could find the troll ship tunnel – then they could just put this electrical cable inside it and the problems would be done and dusted.'

Archie sat back against a warm pipe and rolled a piece of the soft fudge around his mouth.

'You know what?' he said slowly. 'That's not a bad idea …'

Could they work out where the tunnel was? Could they work out how to open it? It was asking a lot, but the three of them had tackled bigger challenges than that. And it wouldn't only help Billy, it would help the whole of Dundoodle. And … perhaps they could find *The Book of the Earth*, with all its magical secrets. Then Archie would become a powerful wyrdworker, learn how to grow an Anyfruit vine and become a brilliant sweet-maker too!

The more he thought about it, the more Archie began to warm to the notion.

The next day, he and Fliss and Billy had a meeting after school, at Clootie Dumpling's café, next door to the McBudge factory. They often went there for Clootie's famous hot chocolate, which was rich and dark and glistened with indulgence.

Archie had been thinking about the tunnel all night, and the possibility that they might be able to open it and find the brownies' precious book. He stirred the little marshmallows into his chocolate excitedly as he told Fliss about Billy's idea.

'I was only joking!' Billy said, but Archie knew he was interested. It would mean delving into Dundoodle's supernatural mysteries, something Billy could never resist.

Fliss, however, frowned.

'I don't know, Archie,' she said. 'This sounds an awful lot like meddling to me. You can't go interfering in people's daily business with your secret magical knowledge. You're meant to be the Tree's guardian, not the town's wizard-handyman. If you go about doing whatever you want, and using magic for your own purposes, you'll end up like Mrs Puddingham-Pye.'

Archie cringed at the mention of his cousin. Mrs P-P and her children, the twins Georgie and Portia, were his arch-enemies and had tried to bump him off so that Mrs P-P could inherit the factory and the Guardianship. She had used her witch magic to help Archie once, but she couldn't be trusted.

'I'm not like her at all!' Archie snapped. 'I'd be helping the town. It'd save a load of money and protect the wildlife from any disturbance. What's the downside?'

Fliss chewed her lip doubtfully. 'What about this *Book of the Earth*?' she said, folding her arms. 'You're going to benefit from that, admit it! If it hasn't turned to mush by now.'

'It's a magic book,' said Billy. 'It would have protection spells woven into it.'

'I want that for the brownies,' said Archie. 'It's *their* book.' But he knew that wasn't quite true. He *would* benefit from it – in fact, maybe it should belong to him? The knowledge was going to be his anyway. His face reddened with guilt.

At that moment, Clootie appeared at their table.

'I'm sorry, Fliss,' she said. 'We can't make your toastie – the sandwich grill's out of order after it blew a fuse when the power came back on yesterday.'

Clootie bustled back to the kitchen, leaving Fliss fuming more fiercely than a piece of burned toast.

'Oh *dear*,' said Archie, drily. 'Whatever shall we do, Fliss?'

'Fine – we'll help with the power supply,' said Fliss, her tummy rumbling discontentedly. 'But I *still* think it sounds a bit dodgy.'

Billy, glad to see his friends had called a truce, dived eagerly into the matter at hand.

'The Fjurge Brownies said the troll captain locked the tunnel,' he said. 'What would he have done with the key?'

'What was his name again?' said Fliss. 'Prong the Pointless?'

'Prang the Pebble-dashed,' replied Archie, taking a folded piece of paper from his schoolbag and laying it across the table. 'I dug out this map of Dundoodle from the library at the Hall. I was searching for places where the tunnel might come out into the loch. There's a rocky stretch on the edge of town that seems like a good candidate. And look what I found ...'

The map was quite detailed, giving the names of streets, woodland and other landmarks. Archie pointed to the label for a section of the loch's shoreline: *Prangstone*.

'I've heard of it,' said Billy. 'It's a slab of rock jutting out over the water like a doorstep. Good work, Archie!'

'And you think Prang might have left the key under that doorstep,' said Fliss, rolling her eyes. 'That's completely bonkers!'

Archie shrugged. 'It's a starting point,' he said. 'And we can easily take a look.'

They finished their hot chocolate and hurried out of the café. If they were going to get to the Prangstone, they had to do it before it got dark.

A group of ladies sat at a nearby table, eating sardines on toast. They watched the children as they left. Where had Archie seen them before? They all looked alike, their dark hair slickly parted around whiskery faces, and their large brown eyes staring wetly at him as he passed their table. Were they sisters? They were dressed alike too, in drab, grey oilskin raincoats.

Then he remembered: the women at Trollhaven! It was odd that he should see them again here so soon afterwards.

One of the women sprang from her chair and pressed a bright-orange flyer into his hand. It had a picture of a sad-looking bird drawn on it.

'Protect our wildlife!' she said, spitting sardine oil from her mouth. 'No digging or other such nastiness in our countryside!'

'OK,' said Archie, slightly startled. 'Um … thanks.'

He hurried after the others. The women were a protest group! That's why they'd been at Trollhaven. They must be keeping an eye on Mr Thaw and his friends.

The three children took Fisherman's Way, the lane

that led to the lochside. Here the road ran alongside a small stony beach with a series of jetties and ramshackle boathouses that leaned over the water, their stilt-like supports casting long, jagged shadows across the loch. In summer, you could hire boats or take fishing trips on its deep, dark waters, but it was too cold and misty for that now.

Beyond the boathouses, heading away from the town, the lane ended. The children were forced to scramble along the shore, which had become rockier and awkward to walk on. Then the land rose into a sheer but shallow cliff, dotted with tufts of grass and frequented by only the occasional daredevil rabbit with a head for heights.

'Prangstone is just round this corner,' said Billy, as they carefully edged along a ledge in the cliff. 'I hope.'

'Don't go slipping over here, Archie,' teased Fliss, 'or you'll make quite a splash.'

Clinging to the rocky wall, and trying not to look at the murky water below, Archie had begun to seriously regret his idea when Billy pointed to a flat wedge of rock a few metres ahead.

'That's it – the Prangstone!'

It did indeed look like a doorstep, a stone shelf hanging over the loch, but there was no sign of any door. Fliss pulled herself up on to its top, dragging the smaller Billy up by the hood of his coat, as Archie studied the underside.

'Nothing but rabbit poo up here!' said Fliss, wrinkling her nose.

'I can't see anything down here either,' Archie said. He tried to keep the disappointment out of his voice. It was unremarkable, merely a smooth slab of rock. This had been a stupid idea. If there was ever a tunnel, the troll captain had no intention of letting anyone find it again.

The sun was now low in the sky, dipping just below the Prangstone.

'What now?' said Fliss.

'We'd better be heading home soon,' said Billy quietly. 'I don't want to be clambering over these cliffs in the dark.'

'Wait a minute …' said Archie.

'What?' said Fliss. 'You've found something, haven't you?'

As the sun lit up the underside of the stone, tiny outlines of symbols had appeared on its surface.

'There are carvings in the rock!' he called up to the others. They were only visible as the sun set, making them cast a shadow that could be seen – the rest of the day they would be hidden in shade.

'What does it say?' said Billy, his voice full of excitement. Archie quickly scanned the inscription. He couldn't understand what all the symbols meant but there was one he *did* recognise.

'There's a symbol of a ship with a small tree growing out of it,' he said. 'It has to be the troll ship – we've found it! We've found the entrance to the tunnel!'

Fliss and Billy hurriedly joined Archie underneath the Prangstone. Billy dragged his notebook out from his school-bag and began copying the strange inscription into it. Then the children hastily retraced their steps across the cliff.

'What does the rest of it mean?' said Fliss, once they'd found themselves back on the safer ground of Fisherman's Way. 'It's just funny-looking stick men.'

'I think these are runes,' Billy said, biting his tongue in concentration as he studied the notebook. 'It's an alphabet that was used in the olden times, as it's easy to carve on rocks or into wood. I'm sure I can find some books that will help me understand what it's saying.'

They were halfway up the dimly lit street when Fliss suddenly stopped.

'What's that?' she said, pointing towards the end of the lane.

A large, menacing shadow blocked their path. It had a bulky body with many heads and legs. As they watched, it moved swiftly towards them and spread, surrounding the children on three sides. Billy grabbed the others' arms, trembling in horror.

'It's an ombrahydra!' he squealed. 'A demonic multi-limbed creature of the twilight – Creepy Scale rating of nine point six-four! It's going to suck out our blood, and chew up our brains, make lacy curtains out of our souls, and … oh, it's only a bunch of ladies in raincoats. Emergency over!'

The shadow was, in fact, several shadows joined together – a huddle of women, staring at the children suspiciously.

'It's the protest group from the café,' said Archie.

'What have we here?' said the woman at the centre of the huddle, who seemed to be their leader. Her voice was cold and calm. 'Children playing by the loch. Very dangerous. Who knows what lurks in its icy, black waters, waiting to drag the unwary to their doom? What might you be up to, instead of being safely tucked up in your cosy homes?'

'None of your beeswax!' said Fliss, indignantly rubbing her arm where Billy had squeezed it. 'Who are you lot anyway? Lurking in shadows and scaring the patooties out of innocent children like us.' She tried to put on an 'innocent' face but couldn't quite manage it, settling for 'witheringly sarcastic' instead.

The woman was taken aback. 'We're spotty,' she said importantly.

'The café food can be a bit greasy,' said Billy sympathetically. 'I have a cream I can lend you.'

'No! S.P.O.T.T.Y. The Society for the Protection of the Tufted Yellowbeak.'

'The tufted *what*?' asked Fliss.

'It's a bird,' snarled the woman. 'And it's very rare. I am Audrey Buttereigh-Krumpitt, the chairperson of our Society. My colleagues and I are here to see the habitat of the Tufted Yellowbeak protected from this monstrous excavation work proposed by the engineers.'

'You mean Mr Thaw and his plans for the electrical cable?' said Archie.

'Indeed. The cable's route over the mountains would go straight through the Yellowbeak's breeding ground. And the noise of blasting a tunnel through the mountains would drown out their distinctive mating calls.

S.P.O.T.T.Y. will protest any construction work to ensure it doesn't happen!'

'So if there was another way to get the cable to Dundoodle, you'd be in favour of it?' said Archie, sneaking a look at the others. Ms Buttereigh-Krumpitt leaned towards him, sniffing the air as if she could smell a secret.

'What do you *mean*, boy?'

'I'm just asking.' Archie had an innocent face that put Fliss's to shame. Ms Buttereigh-Krumpitt's eyes glittered with distrust.

'You should be talking to my mum,' said Billy. 'She's the environmental consultant to the engineers. If you want her help, she'll need to know about your Yellow Tuftybeak.'

'The Tufted *Yellow*beak!' Audrey Buttereigh-Krumpitt barked. 'We shall certainly be having words with your mother, child. Tell her we have rented this boathouse as the headquarters for our protest campaign. The workmen are staying at the Dundoodle Hotel, and we'll be demonstrating outside it until they see sense!'

The women followed her up the steps of one of the rickety buildings that stretched out over the loch. They disappeared through its darkened doorway.

'Do not underestimate us,' she hissed, as the door closed.

The children ran back to the centre of the town, eager to leave the creepy lochside behind them.

'What a bunch of oddballs,' said Fliss. 'Completely bonkers! Mr Thaw has got a fight on his hands against that spotty lot.'

Billy promised to have a go at translating the inscription that evening, and the three of them agreed to meet up after school the next day.

Archie hurried back to the Hall, very pleased with himself and with everything that had happened. There was even more reason to find the tunnel, if it helped a rare bird and stopped a lot of bother between the engineers and the S.P.O.T.T.Y ladies. However, his mood soured when he saw what awaited him at home. A sleek silver car was parked in the drive, next to Mum's battered little hatchback. No one else in Dundoodle had a car like it – Mrs Puddingham-Pye was paying a visit. And that could only mean one thing: trouble.

Archie found Tablet carrying a laden tray towards the library. China cups and saucers and a pile of homemade shortbread wobbled perilously in the old butler's hands as he staggered along the hallway carpet.

'Your mother is having tea with your cousin, Master Archie,' said Tablet, pausing outside the library doors to catch his breath. Archie took the tray from the old gnome, who wheezed gratefully.

'What does *she* want?' he said. At least Georgie and Portia weren't with her, judging from the fact that the hallway was free from bloodstains.

'The latest news in the town is that the Puddingham-Pyes have bought the Dundoodle Hotel, so she's probably come to brag.'

'I didn't know that!' The hotel was where Audrey Buttereigh-Krumpitt had said Gilbert Thaw and the construction team were staying.

'It was sold ages ago, but nobody knew who the buyer was. It's been done up very fancy, I hear,' Tablet said disapprovingly. 'All fluffy scatter cushions, shampoo in tiny bottles and armadillos for breakfast.'

'I think you mean avocados,' said Archie, but you never knew with Mrs Puddingham-Pye.

He took the tray into the library. Jacqueline Puddingham-Pye had folded her long, spiky form into an armchair opposite Archie's mum. Great-Uncle Archibald's portrait glared down at her from above the fireplace. Mum had no idea that she had schemed against Archie, or that the large, black handbag on her lap was occupied by Garstigan, a wicked mobgoblin that she employed as her spy.

Mrs Puddingham-Pye eyed the shortbread disdainfully, as Archie placed the tray on the low table in front of her. If it wasn't made by the Puddingham-Pye Biscuit

Company, it wasn't fit for human consumption.

'Hello, Urchin,' she said, failing to remember Archie's name, as usual. 'Given the servants the day off, have you? Very noble. If you want a job in my new hotel as a waiter or a chimney sweep – or as a footstool, perhaps – then you must let me know.'

'Jacqueline was just telling me about her new business venture,' said Mum, giving Archie a 'best behaviour' warning via the power of a single arched eyebrow.

'Very nice,' Archie said, gritting his teeth.

'You *must* come and visit.' Mrs Puddingham-Pye discreetly smacked away a small scaly claw that was reaching from her handbag to the shortbread plate. Archie heard a muffled muttering from inside.

'Our guests are naturally of the highest quality. We couldn't possibly allow any of the grubbier sorts of people to stay there.'

'You've got some workmen staying there,' said Archie. 'They must be pretty grubby, with their muddy boots and overalls.'

Mrs P-P smiled. It wasn't a nice smile. It was a smile that suggested she knew something Archie didn't.

'Mr Thaw and his friends are performing a public service through their work and are staying at the hotel at my expense. Dundoodle will be transformed by having a stable power supply. A power supply that I'll control.'

'What?' said Archie and his mum together.

'Who do think is paying for the construction work? Puddingham-Pye Biscuits, of course. We're thinking of opening a factory here, and a flour mill – though we'll have to knock down a few streets and shops and things for it. If anyone else wants my electricity, they'll have to pay a premium. Think of the business opportunities, boy!'

Archie stormed out of the library in a fury. Public service, indeed! Mrs Puddingham-Pye was holding the town to ransom. But was that all she was up to? It was never a question of what plots Mrs Puddingham-Pye was concocting, it was more a question of how many.

Now it was even more important to find an alternative way of getting the cable to Dundoodle – to thwart her plans! And, of course, there was *The Book of the Earth* … the thought of it gnawed at Archie's mind.

◄○►

The next morning dawned bright and sunny. The days were getting longer as spring trudged reluctantly into its stride, and the townsfolk of Dundoodle dared to contemplate the possibility of life without thermal underpants.

Archie met Fliss on the way to school.

'It's all kicking off at the Dundoodle Hotel,' she said, grinning. 'Come and have a look – the S.P.O.T.T.Y. ladies haven't wasted any time.'

The entrance to the hotel had been surrounded by a forest of placards, as S.P.O.T.T.Y. staged a protest outside its main entrance. They'd drawn quite a crowd. Archie and Fliss watched from across the street.

DOWN WITH DIGGING, read one banner. **SAY PNO TO PNEUMATIC DRILLS!** read another.

'SAVE THE TUFTED YELLOWBEAK,' Audrey Buttereigh-Krumpitt bellowed through a megaphone. 'PROTECT OUR WILDLIFE FROM NEEDLESS INTERFERENCE!'

The rest of the protestors waved their placards and chorused the slightly catchier rendition: 'We're here! We're S.P.O.T.T.Y.! Our chant will drive you potty!'

Mrs Puddingham-Pye glowered at them from the doorway. This wasn't good for business at all. There were boos as Gilbert Thaw and the other workmen came out of the hotel. Gilbert didn't seem bothered. He gave the children a wave.

'We get this kind of thing all the time,' he said cheerily, crossing the road to join them. The other workmen followed him obediently. 'The S.P.O.T.T.Y. lot have been following us for a while, since the cable project started a couple of years back.'

'Doesn't it upset you?' asked Fliss. 'They don't seem to like you very much.'

'Or the company you keep,' said Archie. 'I heard Mrs Puddingham-Pye's plans for her expensive power supply.'

'It's change that people don't like,' said Gilbert. 'But change happens anyway and people forget how things were before. They forget that they spent time sitting ignorantly in the dark because there was no light. Then light comes along and shows them what they've been missing, and soon they think that's how it always was. It's been the same for thousands of years.'

'I don't think I could be as patient as you,' said Archie, impressed by the man's lack of concern.

Gilbert smiled. 'I've learned to be patient,' he said, as a minibus pulled up at the kerb and the workmen clambered inside it. 'We'd better be going. No rest for the wicked.'

After school, they met up with Billy at the hideout in the factory. He'd been bursting to tell them something all day and didn't even bother to raid Fliss's sweet stash before getting out his notebook.

'I've managed to translate the inscription,' he said breathlessly, flicking through the pages. 'It was quite tricky but I'm pretty sure those runes were carved by Prang the Pebble-dashed himself! It was the actual handwriting of a Viking troll!'

'Brilliant, Billy,' said Fliss. 'I knew you were good for something!'

'What does it say?' asked Archie.

Billy found the page he wanted, cleared his throat – for a bit of extra drama – and read:

'Four guardians watch the Gate,
Sharing the divided key.
Split into its elements,
Hidden from those that we flee.

Seek out the smallest folk's house,
Risk the lair of the watery crones.
Dare the fiery lizards' cave,
Face the old, cold man of the bones.'

'It's a poem,' said Fliss. 'A really bad one.'

'Troll poetry is well known for being terrible,' said Billy. 'You should read *The Saga of Borgo Who Liked to Watch Paint Dry* – it's three thousand verses long and nothing rhymes. But this isn't a poem – it's a riddle! And that's not all … it's a treasure hunt too!'

9

'The inscription is a treasure hunt?' said Fliss. 'How?'

'What does the riddle mean?' asked Archie. They gathered round Billy, reading the lines of the poem to themselves.

'There is a key to open the tunnel,' explained Billy, 'or the Gate, as it's called here. But it sounds like it's been broken into bits and given to different people to look after – the four guardians. The second verse tells you where you have to go to find the different bits.'

'Easy,' said Archie, 'except this was hundreds, maybe thousands, of years ago. Even if we can find all these places, are these four guardians still going to be around now?'

'And why would the troll have gone to so much trouble to hide the key in the first place?' said Fliss. She was still uneasy about the whole idea. 'It's just a key to a stupid tunnel. What's the big deal?'

'There was a fight going on between the gods and the giants,' Archie reminded her. 'The brownies said the troll ship was being chased by a giant. They wanted to make sure no one got through the tunnel and followed them afterwards, so they made it as difficult as possible to reopen it. But the war is long over. There certainly aren't any giants around now.'

Fliss shrugged. 'I still think there's something not right about this,' she said. 'But Billy deserves a reward for his investigations – he can have first pick from the sweet stash.' She reached into the alcove that acted as the sweet store. 'What's this? There's an extra bag in the store. Whose are these Liquorice Bootlaces and other things?'

Archie blushed. 'Those are my rejected sweet-making experiments,' he said. 'I'd forgotten they were there. Give them here and I'll throw them away.'

'I'll have those,' Billy said, grabbing the bag from Fliss and stuffing it into his satchel. 'I never say no to free sweets, rejects or otherwise.'

'You might regret it this time,' said Archie with a grin. 'Don't say I didn't warn you.'

The three children took the passage to Honeystone

Hall, to see if the books in the library could help them with any clues. They found Sherbet snoozing on the sofa in front of the library fire. Tablet arrived with a jug of hot chocolate, as the children discussed the riddle.

'Who are the four guardians of the key?' said Archie, cuddling up to Sherbet on the sofa. *'Dare the fiery lizards' cave*, the riddle says. The fiery lizards – they've got to be the honey dragons, haven't they?'

'It's a good bet,' agreed Billy. 'They have to be magical folk from before the days of the Wyrdie Tree, going back to the ancient times.'

'I thought the Wyrdie Tree was the source of all the magic in Dundoodle,' said Fliss. 'But you're saying there was magic here before that?'

'The world used to be full of magic, young Miss Felicity,' said Tablet, pouring the hot chocolate into mugs. 'But over time it has faded. Most of that which remains around here is earth magic that has the Tree as its source, though there are still a few who date back to the ancient times, like the dragons. They're not sprightly youngsters like me.' He gave a wheezing cackle, before hobbling back to the kitchen.

'If we're looking for people older than Tablet, we should be looking at the fossils in the museum,' sighed Fliss.

'What about the other guardians?' said Archie. 'The "smallest folk", the "watery crones" and the "old, cold man of the bones". Have you any ideas who they might be?'

'I'm not sure,' said Billy. 'Maybe there's a book here on ancient magical people. And the dragons might know who they are.'

'I wouldn't count on the dragons helping much,' Fliss pointed out. 'Apart from Blossom, they're all still in their winter sleep.'

Archie had forgotten that. The honey dragons were hibernating and it was doubtful Blossom would know anything about the key, as she was the youngest of them all. They really needed to speak to Old Jings, who was the only other dragon who knew human speech.

'Maybe we don't need to ask the dragons anything,' he said thoughtfully. 'The riddle says to "dare the cave" – we could just visit the Cavern of Honeystone and have a look around. We wouldn't need to bother the dragons at all.'

'No, Archie!' Fliss was shocked. 'You can't just go into their home and poke around the place whilst they're asleep. It's wrong. How would you like it if someone did that to you?'

'Father Christmas does it,' said Billy flatly.

Fliss gave him a look. Sometimes it was hard to know whether he was being serious or not. 'Unless you're Father Christmas,' she said, 'it is *not* OK.'

'But what about the electricity problems?' said Archie. 'You want to fix them, don't you? Without giving Mrs P-P the satisfaction of making loads of money, that is.'

'Not when the cost is upsetting my friends!'

Archie bit his lip. The honey dragons *had* been good friends to them, and it wouldn't be right to betray their trust. But he so wanted to find *The Book of the Earth*! And the more he thought about it, the more he wanted it – surely the Book's knowledge could solve everything.

'Fine,' he said. 'We'll leave them alone for now. But we'll have to go there eventually if they are one of the guardians.'

'Meanwhile, we need to do some research,' said Billy, scanning the bookshelves. He had spent so much time in the library since Archie had moved to the Hall, he knew its contents better than anyone. 'The riddle mentions "smallest folk" – *seek out the smallest folk's house.'*

'Could it mean the brownies?' asked Fliss. 'They're pretty small.'

'But not the smallest,' said Billy. 'All sorts of wyrdie-people are much smaller – elves, mushroom-squatters, bog fairies and the like. But which is the smallest? It could be difficult to narrow down.

'Let's start with something easier. I'm sure there's a book here that will help ...' He dragged a blue book with a golden sea monster on its cover from one of the shelves. 'Ah, here it is – *The Book of Monstra Aqua!*'

'The book of what?' said Fliss. 'That sounds like a type of shower gel!'

'*Monstra Aqua,*' said Billy with a haughty sniff. He set the book down on the carved oak desk. 'It means "monsters of the water". I thought it might tell us about the "watery crones" whose lair we have to risk.'

'Monsters?' said Archie, giving Sherbet a tummy rub. 'I hope we're not going to have to deal with anything too scary.' Sherbet gave a whine of agreement. Billy was flicking through the book's pages, reading the entries and dismissing various unsuitable creatures.

'The Octopus people ... no, they're only found far out to sea. The Clam Clan ... a family of sea pixies living inside a giant clamshell – don't think so. Prawnzilla ... definitely not. The Selkies ... women who turn themselves into seals – that's too silly. Aha ...'

'What?' said Fliss.

'Mermaids. Of course – the watery crones are mermaids!'

'I know all about them!' said Fliss excitedly. 'Mermaids are beautiful ladies who sing whilst combing their long, golden hair. They wear seashell bikinis and they play all day with their fishy friends amongst the coral.'

'I'm not exactly sure that description fits Saggie Aggie,' said Billy, 'the infamous mermaid of the loch. Creepy Scale rating of seven. She's the only one left. And there's a problem. Just a small, teeny-tiny thing.'

'What?' said Archie.

'Her lair is underwater. How on earth are we going to get there?'

10

As always, Archie's enchanted boat seemed to know where the children wanted it to go. Once it had left the secret cave under Honeystone Hall, it sped across the loch, but away from its usual destination of the old forest.

'Saggie Aggie's lair is supposed to be in a cavern under the island of Wee Greenie,' said Billy.

'That's the direction we're headed in,' said Archie, gazing out over the water with Sherbet at his side. Sherbet loved to ride in the boat and feel the breeze in his fur. 'Hopefully we can get there and back before dark.'

'What are we going to do when we get there?' asked Fliss. 'Paddle around in the hope she passes by? Or does this boat turn into a submarine?'

Archie didn't say anything. He'd been lucky so far, and

it was too much to hope his luck would hold. But Fliss had given him an idea …

Soon they reached Wee Greenie. It wasn't much of an island, unlike the hulk of Pookiecrag with its impressive ruined castle. Behind a veil of thin mist, a cluster of pine trees clung on to a stack of rock, like a sea monster poking its head above the water. The boat stopped a short distance from the edge of the stack, bobbing about expectantly.

'What now?' muttered Billy, clutching his satchel to his chest nervously and peering into the water.

'You're going to have to trust me,' said Archie. 'I'm about to try an experiment.'

'Like your sweet-making experiments?' said Fliss. 'They didn't end well.'

Archie grinned. 'Actually, I'm going to use one of my sweet experiments – Billy, let me have the rejects bag.'

Billy reluctantly took the bag from his satchel. Archie fished around inside it until he found what he wanted.

'My Inflatabubble Gum! Let's see just how inflatable it is!' Archie popped the small pink sweet into his mouth and chewed. Not one to miss out, Billy joined him in trying the gum out. At Archie's signal, they each started blowing a bubble.

The bubbles grew and grew until they covered the entire boat. Eventually they stuck together and merged into one giant bubble.

'Wow!' said Fliss. 'That's amazing! Why did Dad reject these?'

'The problem is they become solid and unchewable,' said Archie, taking the gum from his mouth. 'But that could help us.'

'It's already solid,' said Billy. He tapped the surface of the bubble – although the gum was papery thin, it had become tough like a rubbery balloon. Archie pushed his hands through the bubble, making a large hole. Now that it was solid the bubble didn't deflate and kept its shape. He pulled the bubble around them so that it covered the boat from end to end.

'Are you doing what I think you're doing?' said Fliss. 'You're completely bonkers, Archie McBudge!'

'It was your idea!' Archie chuckled. The next bit would be more difficult. He pointed his fingers at the sides of the boat and concentrated. Billy and Fliss watched as the wooden boat began to sprout leaves. Little branches grew upwards from its prow and encircled the bubble. They intertwined with each other, securing the bubble in place so that it acted as a transparent, airtight shell.

'Archie, you've made a submarine!' Fliss said, laughing with amazement.

'After the brownies gave me the seedling, I wondered if the boat was made from a Spirit Oak too,' said Archie. 'They gave seedlings to my McBudge ancestors – I bet one of them created the boat that way. Anyway, it's responded to my wyrdworking magic spectacularly.'

'But is it safe?' said Billy. 'Is there enough air in here?'

'We'll soon find out,' said Archie. 'Look, we're sinking!'

The boat was merely following their wishes. Would it work? Or would the bubble be crushed and icy-cold water flood in? The children held their breath but there was no sign of any leak.

Fliss couldn't help but gasp as darkness closed over the top of the pink gum roof.

'We're actually underwater!' she said. 'This is amazing – I bet there's never been a submarine in the loch before!'

Although it was dark beneath the loch's surface, there was just enough light to see the shapes of fish darting through the murk around them. The boat moved quickly, diving to where the island rose from the lake floor. Here there was an opening, a mouth-like cave. It did not look very inviting.

Without hesitating, the boat plunged through the

opening, before gently rising again. It surfaced inside a huge cavern.

'We're inside Wee Greenie,' said Archie. 'The island's hollow!' He tore a hole in the bubble and peeked out.

There was a stench of dead fish. The cavern was lit by giant pearl-like lamps that hung from its walls, their feeble glow pale green and sickly. A pillar of rock rose up from the middle of the water in the cavern. Slouched against it sat a hunched, grotesque figure, its wet skin blue and scaly. Two round, cod-like eyes bulged from its

head. Flies buzzed giddily around the creature, which gurgled to itself as it attempted to comb what remained of its hair – a few strands, lank and dark, that fell to its shoulders. It was very different from Fliss's description, but it was definitely a mermaid: a tail like that of a mackerel shone with an oily gleam in the dull light.

'My poor hair,' it sighed pathetically. 'My poor, beautiful hair.'

'It's her!' Archie whispered. 'It's Saggie Aggie!'

'What's that? Who's there?' the mermaid rasped,

peering into the gloom. Her round eyes caught sight of the boat with the three children crouched inside. 'Humans? Children?' She eyed them greedily. 'Breakfast, lunch and dinner all served at once!' She looked at Sherbet and bared her teeth in a nasty smile. 'And a snack for later ...'

Sherbet whined. Had that fish-lady just called him a *snack?*

'You never said she was going to eat us, Billy!' said Fliss. 'That's a rather important piece of information to leave out.'

'There was nothing about that in the old records,' replied Billy, horrified. 'But I suppose those who found out never wrote anything again ...'

The ancient mermaid cackled. She slid her wrinkled body into the water and slowly paddled towards them.

'Oh, you don't need to worry about old Aggie, my dears,' she said. 'I'm only a harmless old fish, living in the dark. I wouldn't harm a fly.' A blue tongue shot out of her mouth and snatched at one of the insects orbiting her head, plucking it out of the air and into her mouth. She swallowed it with one gulp. Billy swallowed a scream.

'W-we were wondering if you could help us,' said Archie, as politely as his nerves would allow.

'What can old Aggie do for you, my dears? Lost your way, perhaps?' She circled the boat lazily, like a shark biding its time. 'There's the stink of magic about you, boy. Who are you?'

'I'm Archie McBudge. I'm the Guardian of the Wyrdie Tree.'

'Pah! The McBudges and their roots-and-mud magic. That's what I could smell! I was here long before them. Before humans and their noise and spears and fishing nets. Before the Tree.'

'I know. And I know you're one of the guardians of the key to the Gate – Prang the troll gave you a part of it.'

'Want it, do you?' The mermaid's eyes flashed slyly. 'You're not the first, boy.'

'Other people have come looking for the key?' The thought hadn't occurred to Archie. 'Who? Why did they want it?'

'Don't know. Don't care. Told them to stop bothering me. Other people's affairs don't interest me and their magic can't harm me, though they tried. Oh yes, they tried.' She cackled again, mischievously. 'Aggie's always been here, my dears. And always will be … combing my lovely hair.'

She stopped, then let out a miserable sob.

'My lovely hair … all gone!' A wail erupted from her spiny-toothed mouth. 'I was so beautiful once! Me and all my sisters were – but now I'm the only one.'

The children watched awkwardly as the monster wept. It was a terrible noise. Archie couldn't help but feel sorry for the creature, as dangerous as she was. What must it be like to live for so long? To be so very, very old and alone?

'There, there,' he said. 'You're still, erm, beautiful.'

'Really?' said Aggie.

'Best looking blue-skinned half-woman, half-fish I've ever seen,' added Billy, trying to be helpful. 'Macabre Loveliness Scale rating of nine point nine nine. Second only to Auntie Doreen.'

'We can help you,' said Fliss. She winked at Archie. What was she up to? 'We can help you with your hair, if you help us with the key.'

Aggie stopped sobbing and eyed the girl uncertainly.

'You'll help old Aggie?'

'In return for your part of the key.'

'A gift for a gift,' the mermaid said to herself. 'That's always been the way of things. And what does Aggie need to look after the silly thing for? No one cares. The giants have crumbled and the gods are long gone. Only Aggie remains. No one cares about old Aggie.'

'I do,' said Fliss. She rummaged in the bag of Archie's rejected sweets and pulled out a handful of the Long-Lasting Liquorice Bootlaces. Her nimble fingers wove them into several neat plaits, which she dangled out of the hole in the bubble. 'Look, it's just your colour too.'

Aggie's eyes widened and a webbed hand reached for the liquorice.

'New hair!' she gurgled with pleasure. 'New hair for Aggie!'

Fliss quickly lifted the bootlaces out of reach.

'Key first,' she said calmly. 'Then the hair.'

The mermaid chuckled. 'Clever girl. Keep your wits about you and you'll live longer.'

With a kick of her tail she returned to the pillar of rock. Hauling herself out of the water, her slippery hands sorted through a pile of bones until she found what she wanted. She swam back to the boat eagerly. In one hand was a slim bottle of black glass filled with a shiny liquid that moved as if it were alive.

'That's part of the key?' said Archie. It wasn't what he was expecting.

'Silver-water,' said Aggie. 'Enchanted water from the well of the gods. Don't ask Aggie how it works. She only looked after it for the silly troll. Where's he now? Turned to dust, probably.'

She flung it roughly through the hole in the bubble, forcing Archie to dive to catch it and making the boat rock wildly. Fliss threw all the liquorice into the water in return. The mermaid grabbed the laces eagerly and draped them over her head.

'Aggie looks so pretty,' she said, admiring her reflection in the water. 'All dressed up and ladylike. Just in time for dinner ...' Her eyes glowed wickedly.

'Time for us to leave,' said Archie, quickly sealing the hole in the bubble. 'Everyone think of home!' The boat immediately submerged, sinking towards the cave's underwater entrance.

'She's following us!' said Fliss.

Behind them, the mermaid's sharp silhouette cut through the gloom. This was her territory and she still had the swiftness of a hunter, despite her age.

'Can't this thing go any faster?' yelled Billy. They raced through the entrance into open water, Aggie giving chase.

Her tail whipped furiously as she put on a burst of speed to catch up with them.

'I hate to mention it, but the bubble is starting to leak,' said Fliss.

'Then *don't* mention it!' squealed Billy. Water was dribbling from the edges of the gum and had started to collect around their feet.

'Hurry, boat!' said Archie, panic rising in him. He could practically feel the craft straining with the effort of keeping ahead, but it wasn't enough. It struggled towards the surface, as more water began to pour in. They were almost in the mermaid's reach. She leered, showing off her piranha-like teeth – she was going to catch them!

'We're doomed!' cried Billy. 'Food for the fishes!'

From out of the shadowy waters around them, a horde of dark shapes emerged, large bodies with fins and tails, barrelling through the murk and circling the boat.

'What now?' said Archie. 'More mermaids?'

'No,' said Fliss. 'Look – they're helping!'

The creatures were charging at Aggie, before veering off at the last moment. The mermaid thrashed angrily at them with her claws but they were too quick for her, staying out of range. They blocked her way in every direction, hurtling around and sending the water into a

spin. Aggie was forced to stop her pursuit, and the gap
between her and her prey widened with every second.
She'd never catch them now!

The boat erupted on to the surface of the loch just as
the bubble collapsed on top of its passengers. They
desperately tore it open, gulping in the fresh air, trying to
rid themselves of the dead-fish stink of Aggie's lair.

Far below, they saw the mermaid glaring at them one last time before she turned and disappeared back into the dark depths of her home.

'We made it!' said Archie, his heart pounding. 'Thanks to … what exactly *were* those things?'

The mysterious, dark shapes had vanished as quickly as they had arrived.

Back in the library of Honeystone Hall, the three children took a closer look at the bottle of silver-water.

'How can this be part of a key?' said Archie, turning the black glass object round in the light of the desk lamp. 'How can you use water to open a door?'

'Perhaps it's a spell?' suggested Billy.

'Or perhaps you use it to water the petunias,' yawned Fliss from the sofa. 'We're not going to know more until we find the other parts.'

'You still want to help, then?' said Archie. 'You were brilliant with Saggie Aggie – the liquorice hair was a stroke of genius!'

'Obviously you can't do this without me,' she said with a smile. 'Those rejected sweets have proved quite useful so far, even if you can't eat them!' She yawned again. 'But that's more than enough adventure for one day. It's time for us to be going home.'

Billy and Fliss left Archie and Sherbet in the library. Archie placed the silver-water bottle inside a box that sat on the library mantelpiece. The box had belonged to Archie's father and was enchanted, so that only a McBudge could open it. It was the safest place to store something valuable. But who else could want such a thing?

Saggie Aggie had said that others had been looking for her part of the key and they'd tried using magic against her to get it. Maybe those people knew about *The Book of the Earth* too and were after its magic spells … Aggie had looked after the bottle for hundreds of years, so it could have happened a long time ago – but what if it hadn't? There might be competition for the key, powerful competition.

Archie felt a sudden sense of urgency – they had to track down the other parts to the key and do it quickly.

Before dinner, he decided to check on his Spirit Oak. By now it was dark outside, and the glass building, with its overgrown tangle of exotic plants, had all the mystery of a wild forest at night. Archie found his way to the young oak by following Sherbet's nose along the path.

'I can hardly see anything in this light,' he said. 'I'll have to come back in the morning.' At his words, a flame appeared in the branch of a tree nearby. It was the little honey dragon using her fiery breath as a torch.

'Thanks, Blossom,' said Archie, as she hopped on to his shoulder. He studied the Spirit Oak by the flickering Dragon-fire.

The sapling had grown a lot since the previous day. It still had that slight wonkiness Billy had noticed, from when the pot had broken, but Archie was sure it would sort itself out. Its smooth trunk had broadened and flattened, and there were more leaves budding from its sides.

The brownies had said the tree would sense Archie's need, and it appeared it already knew what that was, even though Archie didn't have a clue himself. Maybe it could feel his worries about the treasure hunt, and was growing into something that would help him?

SOON.

The voice! It had been quiet for a couple of days, and it was much less powerful than when Archie had heard it in Trollhaven. A single word – it was almost as if the voice wanted to remind Archie that whoever was speaking was still around somewhere and hadn't gone away. Was it connected to the tunnel? And if so, how?

He realised the flame had gone out and they were sitting in the dark.

'Have the other dragons woken up yet?' he asked.

'Not yet,' Blossom said in her husky voice. 'Still sleepy-times. But not long now.' In spite of his worries, Archie would have to wait.

◆◯◆

In his geography lesson the following day, Archie absently doodled dragons and ships and sweet-making trees in his notebook. There was far too much to think about to pay attention to Mr Fingle as he introduced the class to the delights of the water cycle, the main outcome of which was to make everyone aware of just how full their bladders were.

'No, Ewan Fothergill!' said the exasperated teacher. 'You may not go to the toilet *again*! You will have to wait until break.'

'But sir,' whimpered Ewan, crossing his legs. 'I can't help it. It's all this talk of trickling and flowing and dripping…' This prompted several other hands to shoot up.

'And in science class earlier,' Fliss piped up helpfully, 'Mrs McGinty said all humans were about sixty per cent water. Imagine all that sloshing around inside us! We're just great big bags of liquid ready to burst and gush all over the place.'

'For goodness sake!' said Mr Fingle, glaring at Fliss as even more hands went up. 'Fine – we'll have a class toilet break. Everyone back here in five minutes!'

The classroom emptied, leaving only Archie, Fliss and Billy. Billy looked thoughtful.

'All this talk about being made of water has given me an idea,' he said.

'Then go to the loo with everyone else,' said Fliss.

'No – not that! It's about the treasure hunt.'

They gathered round his desk.

'Quickly,' said Archie. 'We've only got a few minutes.'

'The riddle says the key has been *split into its elements*,' said Billy. 'And one of the parts of the key is water, or at least, magical water.'

'So?' said Fliss.

'In ancient times, people thought that everything was

made from four elements – water, air, fire and earth.'

'The brownies said something about that,' said Archie. 'The magic of the Wyrdie Tree is a type of earth magic.'

'So maybe the four parts of the key relate to the four elements. We have water from the watery crone already.'

'And perhaps the dragons have something fiery as their part of the key,' suggested Fliss. 'That's brilliant, Billy! So what about the other two elements?'

'Remember when we were on the bus to Trollhaven, and Mr Fingle pointed out a stone circle?'

'That pile of rocks?'

'He called it Gorm's Bones.'

'You think Gorm could be the old man of the bones from the riddle?' said Archie. '*Face the old, cold man of the bones.* But what has that to do with the elements?'

'There's another name for that stone circle,' said Billy, smiling. 'Its original name. The ancients knew it as the Temple of the Air …'

There weren't that many bus stops on the mountain road between Dundoodle and Trollhaven, as sheep were not, by and large, frequent users of public transport. The usual travellers on this route were rugged hikers and tough mountaineers. The three passengers on the bus certainly did not fit that description.

'Do you know where you're going?' asked the driver suspiciously, as he let Archie and the others off at the closest stop to Gorm's Bones.

'We're doing a project on the stone circle,' said Fliss, observing the truth from a distance. 'We shan't be long.'

'The Dundoodle bus stops here in half-an-hour's time,' warned the driver, who was wise to the ways of schoolchildren. 'And it's the last one of the day. Project or not, you youngsters make sure you're on it. The weather here is unpredictable and can change in an instant.'

He wasn't wrong. As the children scrambled over the rough, rocky ground, the blustery wind dropped suddenly. Rivers of mist slunk up the valley and swirled at their feet, making it difficult to know where to tread.

After walking uphill for a difficult few minutes, they found themselves on a flattened stretch of ground at the base of an ice-scarred mountain.

'Gorm's Bones,' said Billy, pointing to four fingers of stone that poked up from the fog. 'A place of worship from the dark, dark ages.'

'Have you noticed how silent it is?' said Fliss. Her voice had dropped to a whisper as they approached the circle. 'It almost hurts. No sounds of water, or sheep, or even a Beaky Yellowtuft.'

'Tufted Yellowbeak,' corrected Archie. 'It is very spooky. Like the rocks are gravestones in an old cemetery.'

'Don't say that!' said Billy, clutching Archie's sleeve. 'We only narrowly escaped getting eaten by an overgrown pilchard with attitude yesterday. Who knows what we're going to find here.'

The stones had looked small from the road, but from this distance, the children could see they were huge. Each block of melancholy grey rock was the height of a house and covered in dry scabs of lichen.

They stepped warily into the circle, the stones looming over them. In the middle of the circle a fifth stone, hidden by the mist, lay flat upon the ground, like an enormous table.

'Now what?' said Archie. 'This is the Temple of the Air. So we need to find ... some air?'

There was a soft, echoing groan and a rippling movement through the mist, as if the mountain itself was breathing out. On top of the central stone, the vapour stirred purposefully and slowly took shape.

'Creepy Scale rating of eight point two and rising!' hissed Billy. 'What is it?'

'Who dares to enter the temple?' the apparition croaked. It was an old man dressed in a long robe. His beard grew to his waist, and his lined face was painted with strange markings. 'Be gone, trespassers,' he said, angrily, 'or suffer the wrath of the spirits who dwell here!'

Billy and Fliss backed away.

'Do we have any sweets to bribe him with?' said Billy. 'Do ghosts eat Jelly Teddies?'

'Be gone, I say!' the spirit bellowed, shaking its fists at them. 'Boo!' it added, unconvincingly.

Archie stood his ground. 'Sorry,' he said, a little uncomfortably, 'but I've seen a ghost before. My great-uncle, in fact. We talk occasionally. Perhaps you know him?'

The phantom sighed and sat down on the stone. It looked very tired.

'Typical!' it said. 'How am I supposed to haunt a place when ghosts are having nice little chats with their relatives? I'm sure that's against the rules. Either way, it's very frustrating, after all my effort with the mist and everything.'

'Are you Gorm?' asked Billy, moving closer. 'Were you the priest of the Temple of the Air?'

'The Temple of the *Winds*, actually. There is one stone for each of the four winds. But some clever clogs asked if that meant we worshipped Brussel sprouts – very disrespectful – and so it had to be renamed the Temple of the Air to stop people from laughing.'

'What's the fifth stone for?' Archie asked.

The ghost looked embarrassed.

'It was my idea. A stone to represent the most powerful wind, the storm wind that blows through the valley from the sea. It was meant to stand in the centre of the circle, the greatest stone of all. It took a hundred men to raise it upright.' He patted its weathered surface.

'What happened?' said Fliss.

'It blew over,' snapped Gorm. 'In a storm. And unfortunately, I happened to be right underneath it. Gorm the Ironically Flattened, they called me. Anyway, I've been here ever since, my bones stuck under this rock. Failing in death, just as in life.' He folded his arms sulkily.

'Gorm the gormless, more like,' muttered Fliss.

'I'm really sorry to hear that,' Archie said to the ghost. 'But you wouldn't be failing if you could help us – we're looking for the key of Prang the troll. We think he might have given you one of its elements to look after.'

'Oh yes, the war of the gods and giants,' said Gorm. 'Nasty business. Some of the giants were made in these very mountains.'

'Made?' asked Fliss. 'What do you mean? I thought giants were just overgrown people.'

The ghost laughed. 'Certainly not! Giants are constructed, built, quarried. They're inanimate objects of stone or clay or wood, given life by magic. They were weapons.'

'I had no idea,' said Billy, pulling his notebook from

his bag. 'This will be a whole chapter in my *Book of Wyrdiness.*'

'The brownies didn't mention that,' said Archie. 'They just said that the warlocks had promised the giants eternal life, if they did what they were told.'

'The warlocks are the ones who *made* the giants,' Gorm said. The ex-priest looked pleased to have an interested audience. 'The most talented of the warlocks was Waterblight the Giant-smith. He made loads of giants for the war. But they were difficult to control, even for the warlocks, so promises were made to ensure they did their masters' bidding. Who knows if the warlocks would have kept their promise? All the giants were destroyed, of course – the gods saw to that. Then they punished the warlocks for their impertinence, stripping them of their magic and dooming them to wander the world, powerless forever. Though there are tales that Waterblight managed to hang on to some of his craft.'

Archie looked at his watch. They would have to get back to the road soon or they would miss the bus. And it was a long walk back to Dundoodle.

'So now that Prang's key doesn't need to be hidden any more,' he said, 'perhaps you wouldn't mind giving it to us? You were the guardian of the air element, weren't you?'

'Ah, the Breath of Maldemer,' replied Gorm, nodding. 'A flask of the sea breeze, summoned by the god of the sea himself. Prang gave it to me, you're quite correct.'

'Then you'll give it to us?'

'No,' the ghost said flatly.

'Why not?' said Archie desperately. 'We've been to a lot of trouble over this and we really, really need it.'

'I can't,' said Gorm. 'I'm sorry, but I've already given it to someone else.'

'Who did you give the flask to?' said Archie. 'And when?'

His fears had been realised – somebody else was after the key. They must be looking for *The Book of the Earth* too!

'It was recently,' Gorm replied irritably. 'I'm afraid I don't have a good sense of time passing. Days become years very quickly when you're in the afterlife.'

'Can you remember who you gave it to?' Fliss said gently.

'A woman. A magical sort. She was very demanding. I didn't take to her at all, but she was insistent. So I gave her the flask, just to make her go away.'

'He must mean Mrs Puddingham-Pye!' said Billy. The others nodded. She certainly fitted the description.

'Saggie Aggie said that magic was used when someone tried get the bottle of silver-water,' he continued, 'and Mrs P-P is the only person we know who can do that.'

'But why does she want the key?' wondered Fliss.

'Maybe she's trying to find the tunnel for the same reasons as us,' said Billy, 'to get the electric cable here with the least amount of fuss, particularly from those annoying S.P.O.T.T.Y. ladies. And it would mean even more profit for her.'

'Or she's after *The Book of the Earth*,' said Archie, with panic in his voice.

'That's what this is all about, isn't it, Archie?' snapped Fliss. 'The Book! That's what you're really bothered about!'

Archie scowled.

'That's not true!' he said. 'If she's after the Book, then it's for a bad reason and we should be worried.'

'We can take comfort knowing that she doesn't have the silver-water,' said Billy. 'But also *we* can't do anything without the Breath of Maldemer. We're stuck.'

'Maybe,' said Archie. 'Or maybe we should pay the Puddingham-Pyes a visit.'

'We'd better get a move on,' said Fliss. 'The bus will be going past soon.'

The bus!

Thanking the old ghost, they ran back across the mist-covered mountainside and just made it to the stop in time. The driver dropped them off in the centre of the town, outside the Dundoodle Hotel. Archie marched towards the building's entrance. A cluster of S.P.O.T.T.Y. ladies were keeping guard but he brushed past their disapproving faces.

'What are you going to do?' said Fliss, running to keep up. 'I can't help thinking this is going to be another bad idea of yours.'

'I'm going to talk to Mrs Puddingham-Pye,' Archie said. 'I don't see what else we can do.'

∗◐∗

The three children pushed their way through the revolving doors into the hotel lobby. It was very grand, and had obviously had a substantial portion of the Puddingham-Pye fortune spent on it. Ornate wood panelling was reflected in gilded mirrors and sparkling chandeliers hung over spotless marble floors. There didn't seem to be anyone about, either at the reception desk or on the plush sofas dotted around the room.

Archie rang the bell on the desk. There was silence for a moment, then a pair of unwelcoming faces appeared from behind it: Georgie and Portia Puddingham-Pye! They smirked at the visitors.

'We're full,' said Georgie. 'Go away.'

'I don't want a room,' said Archie. 'Where's your mum?'

'Mummy's busy talking to Gilbert,' said Portia. 'So we're in charge. Now go away and take your weird friends with you.'

'We want to talk to her about the tunnel,' said Fliss. 'And Gilbert Thaw's digging.'

'Oh, that,' said Portia, whose finger was buried in her nose with an excavation project of its own. 'And why would she want to talk to boring dweebs like you? Mummy knows what she's doing. And if anyone's an expert on dynamite it's me and Georgie, after that incident with the bank vault in Invertinkle.'

'Does she really want to use dynamite?' said Archie. 'What if it damages *The Book of the Earth*?'

'What book? Who cares about any silly book! Mummy wants to make a new road. They're saying the tunnel's for an electrical cable, because that doesn't sound so bad. But actually they're going to blast an enormous hole through the mountains, far bigger than they need for a cable.'

'It'll practically be a new valley,' said Georgie.

'Then Mummy will use a bit of magic to make it look like there's been a convenient earthquake or landslide or something, so it will look like an accident, but it will be too late for anyone to do anything about it. And it'll be so huge we can put all the cables we want in it, charge loads of money for the electricity and build a great big road for the cars and trucks going to our new factory.'

'We'll be even richer than before,' smirked Georgie.

Archie's jaw dropped. Mrs Puddingham-Pye was ambitious, that was for sure.

'What about the key?' said Billy. 'Doesn't she want Prang's key?'

The twins looked at them blankly.

'A key?' said a voice behind Archie's ear. Mrs Puddingham-Pye had an unnerving habit of sneaking up on people. She leaned over his shoulder. 'Did you want a room here, Urchin? Honeystone Hall *is* a bit of a wreck. The cobwebs almost hold the place together. I don't blame you for wanting a night away.'

'No—' began Billy.

'Yes,' Archie interrupted him. 'Yes, please. I heard so much about the hotel that I wanted to see what it was like – if you don't mind giving us a tour?'

'I'm sure the twins would be *delighted* to show you around,' Mrs P-P purred.

Georgie and Portia's blotchy, pouting faces clearly suggested they were thinking the exact opposite.

'Take a key card to the Jacqueline Suite, our premier room. Mr Thaw is staying in it at the moment, but I'm sure he wouldn't mind you having a quick peek.'

The twins groaned a protest, but took the magnetic key and led the others to the lift.

'Why did you stop me talking to her about Prang's key?' Billy whispered to Archie.

'I'm not exactly sure,' said Archie. 'There's something odd going on. Odder than usual for the Puddingham-Pyes.'

Inside the lift they found Garstigan the mobgoblin wearing an apron and carrying a feather duster.

'Where are the bratlings off to?' the creature snarled, flapping its leathery wings. 'Visiting the spa for a beauty treatment, perhaps? Garstigan has formulated a special face mask for greasy boils.'

'It gives you greasy boils, you mean,' said Georgie, as

the lift whisked them upwards. 'We're going to the fourth floor, to Gilbert's room.'

Garstigan grimaced.

'Messy boots and muddy footprints everywhere! Garstigan spends all day cleaning up after him and his friends.'

'Don't worry,' said Portia. 'They'll be gone soon. The last of the dynamite is planted in the mountains tomorrow. Once the charges have been laid ...'

Georgie laughed with relish. 'Tomorrow night everything goes BOOM!' he said.

At the fourth floor, Garstigan fluttered out of the lift, followed by the children.

'Go and clean Room 423,' Portia ordered him, pointing down the corridor. 'Georgie and I had a little accident in there. It turns out watermelons explode quite spectacularly if you throw an axe at them hard enough.'

The creature disappeared along the passage, muttering complaints under his breath, as Georgie tried the key card in a door with the name *Jacqueline* written on it in curly gold letters. He hadn't even taken the key out before the door opened and Gilbert Thaw's face appeared in the doorway. Mr Thaw frowned angrily.

'What are you kids up to?' he said. Then he saw Archie and his face softened. 'Oh, it's you lot.'

'Sorry,' said Fliss. 'We didn't mean to disturb you. We just wanted to look at the room.'

'It's a bit plush for me, to be honest,' admitted Gilbert with a smile, throwing the door back and letting them in. 'The boys and I were having a meeting about the work we did today.' The workmen were all standing about in the room, watching them silently.

'Would that work be something to do with dynamite?' said Archie. 'A lot more dynamite than anyone thinks you're using … ? You're going to blow up a mountain, from what we've heard.'

Gilbert looked surprised for a moment, then frowned again.

'Listen, kids,' he said, his voice taking on a threatening growl. 'This is business between me and Mrs P. Once the work is done, everything will be different. Everything will be better – I'll see to that.'

'What's to stop us from telling?' said Fliss. 'The S.P.O.T.T.Y. ladies would love to know that there'll be nothing but a pile of rubble left for the Buffy Leakytail.'

'The Tufted Yellowbeak,' Gilbert said. The man leaned towards her, his big hands folding into fearsome-looking fists. There was a scar like a large bite mark on his arm. He suddenly looked very dangerous. 'Telling tales would not be a good idea. Me and the boys would not be very happy. And the boys get funny ideas about rearranging people's body parts when they are unhappy.'

The silent workmen glared at them. There was an alarming flicker in their eyes, as if a fire burned furiously behind their expressionless faces.

'I think we'd better go,' said Billy.

'Very wise,' said Gilbert, as they filed out of the room. 'And you'd be even wiser to forget what you've heard today.'

Fliss's face was red with anger as they stepped out on to the darkening street.

'What a horrible man!' she said. 'I want to be an engineer, but I certainly don't want to be an engineer like that! To think I kept that business card he gave me at the beach.' She pulled the card from her pocket and tore it into little bits, which she shoved into her bag.

'Now what do we do?' said Billy.

'We need to think,' said Archie. 'Let's go to Clootie's for a hot chocolate before dinner. It's half past five, so we've just got time.'

The cosy little café seemed a world away from the dreary cavern in the lake, the haunted stones and even the luxurious hotel. It felt like nothing bad could happen at Clootie Dumpling's, but the children sat round their usual table with grim faces.

'I don't understand what's going on,' said Billy. 'Why would Mrs Puddingham-Pye be helping Gilbert blast a tunnel through the mountains? If she's been looking for the elements for Prang's key, she already knows the Gate is there.'

'It's a waste of her time and money,' agreed Fliss.

'But what if she doesn't know there's a tunnel there?' said Archie. 'She doesn't know the story of the Wyrdie Tree – the brownies wouldn't have told her. They don't have anything to do with her. And did you see the look on the faces of the Puddingham-Piglets when you mentioned Prang? And *The Book of the Earth*? They hadn't got a clue what we were talking about.'

'Maybe they were all lying,' said Fliss. 'What magical woman could Gorm have spoken to, other than Mrs P-P?'

'I don't know,' admitted Archie.

'And isn't it odd that they want to blast a hole exactly where the troll tunnel is?' said Billy. 'That can't be a coincidence, can it?'

'I don't know the answer to that either,' said Archie, hitting the table in frustration so that their hot chocolate mugs jumped. The café's other customers turned to look at him. He lowered his voice. 'But I know that finding *The Book of the Earth* is going to be impossible if it's buried under piles of rock with trucks driving over it. What is Mrs Puddingham-Pye thinking? We have to find the remaining parts of the key before she blows the whole thing to pieces tomorrow evening!'

'We have one part – the element of water,' said Fliss, counting them off on her fingers. 'The honey dragons probably have another – the element of fire. The mysterious magic-woman has the element of air. According to the riddle in the inscription, we need to *seek out the smallest folk's house* – that's where the last element will be.'

'I've been racking my brains these last couple of days,' said Billy, his head in his hands. 'There are so many "small folk" in the magical world – the toe-biters of Glen Ferret, the mini-men of the lost valley, the iron dwarfs of Ben Bogie, the micro-elves of Greeniewood … If you want small, cute and pointy-eared – and occasionally vicious and bloodthirsty – magical folk, you're spoilt for choice around here.'

'Come on, Billy,' said Archie. 'We're running out of time!'

Fliss grabbed her mug, before Archie could start hitting the table again. At that moment, Clootie Dumpling passed by carrying a jug of hot chocolate.

'Did you want a top-up, dears?' she asked, her eyes a-twinkle as usual. Clootie always seemed to know when chocolate was required.

'We've got to go for dinner soon,' said Fliss, holding out her mug. 'So perhaps only a tiny smidgen.'

Billy looked up as Clootie smiled and poured a generous helping of chocolate into Fliss's mug.

'What did you just say?' he whispered, as Clootie moved on.

'A smidgen. I can't eat my dinner if I'm full up on the sweet stuff.'

'That's it!' Billy stood up. 'I know who the smallest folk are!'

'Who?' said Archie.

'The Smidgenfolk! They're the *smallest* of the small folk. Creepy Scale rating of four point six. Families of tiny people – they lived in burrows in the ground. That would fit with the earth element of the key. But there's been no rumour of them for years. I think they're extinct.'

'Do you know where their burrows were? Even if they're not around, the last element of the key might still be there.'

'I do know,' said Billy, a worried look on his face. 'But it was destroyed years ago. The location was cleared and flattened for a new building.'

'Which building?'

'The McBudge Chocolate Factory.'

16

Archie's face fell.

'Oh no!' said Fliss. 'If the House of the Smidgenfolk was destroyed, then their part of the key must have been destroyed too.'

'I'm sorry, Archie,' said Billy.

Archie stared miserably into his mug. There was a long silence. Then he looked up, his eyes brightening. 'I don't believe it,' he said firmly.

'What?' said Fliss.

'The House of the Smidgenfolk can't have been destroyed. The McBudges who built the chocolate factory knew about magic – the secret ingredient of McBudge Fudge is honeystone made by the honey dragons, after all!'

'So?'

'The McBudges are guardians of magic – there's no way they would have trashed the home of wyrdie-folk on purpose. It's not the McBudge way.'

'Perhaps it was an accident?' suggested Billy.

'Or perhaps the House is still there. Remember the secret cave by the loch, and the passageway that leads down to it? I've always thought there might be other secret, hidden tunnels in Honeystone Hall somewhere. Maybe there are some under the factory too!'

'It's worth a look,' said Billy. He glanced out the window at the dark street. 'The factory workers are all going home for the day. It'll soon be empty – the ideal time to check your theory.'

'But we have to be getting home too,' said Fliss. 'That's not fair!'

Archie grinned. 'I'll let you know if I find anything,' he said.

∞○∞

After dinner, Archie let himself into the factory using the door from the house. He flicked on a row of switches and yellow light blinked on to the deserted workplace.

'Where to start?' he said aloud. The machines and conveyer belts were silent.

First, he studied the floor for manhole covers, then drainage grates and loose flagstones. He spent an hour walking around the factory but without seeing any signs of a secret passage.

Then he remembered there was a cellar. He had never visited it, as it was mostly used for storage and filled with boxes. He located the door labelled *Basement*, which opened on to a metal staircase that descended into darkness.

Archie had found the factory quite spooky when he first arrived in Dundoodle, with its tangle of metalwork and machinery, strange noises and smells, and its maze of gangways, workshops and kitchens. He had quickly learned to love the place, though, and usually felt no fear being there on his own. But now even he hesitated in the doorway.

There was magic here, he could sense it. He ought to be careful, but each step downwards announced his arrival to anyone lurking with an echoing *clank*.

Fliss would have brought a torch with her, he thought. *Why am I never prepared?*

In the cellar, he could make out the shapes of the storage boxes, a mountain range of blocks stretching into the shadows. He took one step forward. There was a scratching sound from nearby. Mice? He stopped in his tracks and the noise stopped.

He took another step forward. The scratching began again.

Something was here, and it was watching him.

'This is creepy,' he said. Without a light, he had little chance of finding any secret passages. He turned to go, and walked face-first into a mass of writhing, spindly, hairy legs.

'Arrggh!' he cried, clawing at the air in front of him, as the legs batted against his nose. An enormous, hairy spider had dropped down from the ceiling in front of him. It was larger than any he'd ever seen and dangled before his face menacingly. Horrified, Archie took such a deep intake of breath that he sucked the creature into his mouth.

He spat the wiggling legs out. 'Yuck!'

'Arrggh!' the spider said, pushing itself away from him. 'Yuck yourself!'

Archie staggered backwards. Was he hearing voices again? 'Y-you spoke!' he said to the spider.

'I thought I was about to be eaten!' it replied furiously. 'Mum would have gone mad! I hope you haven't ruined my clothes with your stupid drool.'

Archie stepped closer. In the light from the doorway above he could see the spider was, in fact, a tiny girl in a spider costume, complete with extra-furry legs and a hood covered in beady, pretend eyes. Her belt was attached to a rope as fine as spider silk, from which she swung precariously as she tried to untangle two of her spare legs.

'You're a girl!' said Archie. 'A very small one, that is.'

'Well done, genius. And size is relative, I might add. This outfit usually works on the big folk, if they come down here when we're working. There's one called Fiona who runs for her life at the sight of me. Gobkin does a great impression of her scream.' The girl stopped to chuckle at the memory.

'Are you one of the Smidgenfolk?' asked Archie. 'I've been looking for you.'

The girl eyed him warily, trying to work out if he was trustworthy or not.

'You're the McBudge boy,' she said eventually. 'We've seen you about. I thought it was you, otherwise I would have been more careful. But I guess you've encountered quite a few unusual things by now.'

'I'm Archie. I need your help.'

'I'm Gafferty. Gafferty Sprout. And as for helping you, you'll have to ask Mum and Dad. But if you get me down from here, I'll put in a good word for you.'

Archie couldn't help but admire Gafferty's self-confidence, considering she was so much smaller than him. He put out his hand so the girl could stand in his palm. Now that she wasn't swinging from side to side, she was able to sort all her legs out. Then she unhooked her belt from the rope and adjusted a bulky bag hanging from her back.

'That's better,' she said. 'Now, take me over to that

shelf, if you wouldn't mind.' Running along the wall, at about Archie's eye height, was a shelf heavy with large jars of syrup. He gently carried the girl over to the shelf and raised his hand so she could easily jump across to it.

'There's a light switch just behind you,' she said.

Archie flicked the switch.

The cellar was a reassuringly plain room, filled with things that might be useful for a sweet factory: supplies of chocolate chips, food colouring and sacks of sugar. He watched as Gafferty ran along the shelf to the far end of the cellar.

Archie realised that the cellar was L-shaped, but one part was hidden by a towering stack of boxes that blocked it off at the corner. Gafferty dived into a gap between two of the boxes. She disappeared for a moment and then her tiny face reappeared.

'Come on,' she said. 'Welcome to the House of the Smidgenfolk!'

The boxes were heavy, so Archie had to nudge one little by little, until there was enough space for him to clamber through. Behind it, and round the corner, were some shallow steps that led down to an iron gate which barred the way into a dark tunnel. Gafferty had slipped under the gate.

'It's open,' she said. 'No one ever comes down here. Everyone thinks it's a maintenance access point for the water pipes.'

Opening the gate, Archie again felt the presence of magic. It was getting closer. He followed the Smidgen-girl as she scampered down the passageway, her four extra spider legs bobbing about as she ran.

'I was told the House of the Smidgenfolk was destroyed

when they built the factory,' Archie said.

Gafferty laughed. 'That's what everyone was supposed to think. But it's still here. There just aren't many Smidgenfolk left to use it.'

There were lights along the wall of the passage at Archie's ankle height, so Gafferty could see her way easily but Archie had to feel his way along the tunnel as it went deeper into the ground. Eventually it opened out into a cave filled with a warm, welcoming light.

'I knew there must be other caves underneath the factory!' Archie said.

'There's a whole network of them in Dundoodle, with exits in all kinds of places. The Smidgenfolk know most of them. We use them for travelling about the town without getting stepped on. Here we are – home.'

Archie saw that in one wall of the cave the stone was cut with many square holes – windows that were the source of the light. It was a building – a tower block for Smidgenfolk – but only as tall as an adult human. It had been carved out inside the rock, caves within caves, a city in miniature. Archie was reminded of a beehive, or an ant farm he had seen in a museum once.

Gafferty disappeared inside a tiny doorway on the ground, and Archie could follow her movements up a set of Smidgen-sized stairs inside. It was like watching the goings-on in a doll's house! There were many rooms complete with furniture, but a greater number were empty and looked like they had been that way for years.

'Mum! Dad! We've got a visitor!' Gafferty called.

A muddle of voices answered: some were hushed, surprised and concerned, but a younger voice one was loud and excited. Seconds later, a cluster of little people assembled on a balcony at Archie's eye level.

A miniature man examined him sternly whilst carrying the tiniest – and most unimpressed – baby Archie had ever seen. Next to him stood a woman who smiled nervously and a boy, younger than Gafferty, whose eyes popped out of his head at seeing one of the big folk outside his window. Archie noticed their unusual clothing. They were all dressed to resemble insects or creepy-crawlies of one kind or another. The man's clothes took the form of a dusty brown beetle, with an overcoat like its wing case, and the woman's spotted shawl gave her the appearance of a ladybird. The boy resembled a blue and green grasshopper, whilst the baby looked like a slug.

'This is the rest of the Sprout clan,' said Gafferty, joining them. She had removed her extra legs and was untying the bag from her back. 'My mum and dad, Gloria

and Gumble, and my younger brothers, Gobkin and Grub.' She turned to her parents. 'This is Archie. He's the McBudge heir.'

'Pleased to meet you, Archie,' said Gloria. 'I hope our Gafferty hasn't given you any trouble.' At that moment Gafferty tipped up her bag, sending its contents everywhere.

'Chocolate chips!' squeaked Gobkin, happily picking up a lump of chocolate in each hand.

'Did you pinch those from the factory?' said Archie, grinning.

'We don't pinch, we *borrow*,' said Gafferty.

'No, we pinched them,' admitted Gumble gruffly. 'But it's not like the big folk will miss a few wee chocolate chips.'

'It's fine,' said Archie. 'In fact, I have a favour to ask you.'

'We'll happily help the McBudges,' said Gloria. 'They built the factory over this land years ago to protect and hide the House of the Smidgenfolk. There was talk of digging the ground up to mine the rocks, but the McBudges put a stop to that! There were lots of families all living here together then. The noise and the bustle! It must have been very merry. Sadly there aren't so many of us now, and most have moved on, but the Sprouts have stayed true to the House.'

Archie gave them an understanding smile. It was a bit like Honeystone Hall and its many empty, dust-filled rooms. He had only been there a year or so, but it was definitely home and he couldn't imagine living anywhere else.

'I'm looking for the key of Prang the troll,' he said. 'There are different parts to it, and I think he left a part of it with the Smidgenfolk for safekeeping, hundreds of years ago.'

Gloria looked at Gumble uncertainly.

'I've never heard of such a thing,' she said. Gumble shrugged.

Archie looked about the cave. 'My powers are linked to earth magic,' he said. 'I can feel it here, now. This section of the key is formed from the earth too – I bet that's what I'm sensing.'

'The Smidgenfolk were numerous and proud in the ancient times,' said Gloria. 'But so much has been lost – both knowledge and people. If anyone did know about this key, they didn't pass it on.'

'We're still proud,' said Gumble, 'and we'll help, if we can. What does the thing look like?'

'I don't know,' said Archie. 'Something made of earth or stone, something unusual or out of place …' He paced the cave, scanning the floor, trying to make out the source of the magic that he was so sure was close by.

'The summer house!' said Gafferty. She vanished from the balcony and reappeared a few moments later outside. She pointed to a stalagmite growing up from the floor of the cave. 'That's what we call it, though the seasons don't change down here. It's hollow inside, so we use it as a den to play in. There's only room in it for Gobkin and me. I always thought it was odd because it's the only one in the cave.'

Archie's bigger stride meant he got to the stalagmite before the others. It wasn't attached to the ground as a stalagmite should be, but rested on a circular wall of small stones. Its surface was engraved with a fine swirling pattern. He picked the stone up and turned it around, holding it like a large ice cream cone. Instantly, he felt a tingling surge of energy channel from his hand and rush through his body.

This was it, he was sure of it – the earth element of the troll captain's key!

18

'Hey! That's our summer house!' Gobkin burst into tears. 'You can't steal it!'

'I'm sorry,' said Archie awkwardly. 'I'm only going to steal ... *borrow* it for a while. I'll bring it back when I can.' He remembered the rejected sweets. They were in his pocket – he'd taken them back from Billy after the incident with Aggie, after they'd proved so useful. 'How about a Jelly Teddy in return? Chips-and-curry-sauce flavour?' he asked hesitantly.

Gobkin's face lit up.

'Chips and curry sauce! Yes, please!'

'There's a tunnel to McGreasy's Burgers that is well worn from all our visits,' laughed Gloria.

'I'm glad someone shares my taste,' said Archie,

handing over a Jelly Teddy to Gobkin, who hugged it tightly. He liked the Smidgenfolk. They might be the smallest ancient magical folk, but they were also the nicest.

They walked back towards the passageway that led to the factory.

'Thank you for your help,' Archie said. 'And I promise the McBudges will continue to protect the House as best they can.'

They waved him off as he made his way back up to the cellar, carefully carrying the stone. Archie's hunch about the Smidgenfolk, along with Billy's expert knowledge, had proved correct. He felt a lot more hopeful about finding the key than he had when they were sitting in the café earlier. They had two of the four parts, and a good lead on the third. But what about the fourth, the Breath of Maldemer? Did Mrs Puddingham-Pye have it, after all? Time was running out, if they were going to open the tunnel before she blew it to bits the following night.

Back at the Hall, Archie was greeted by Sherbet. The dog sniffed him suspiciously.

'What's the matter, boy?' Archie said. 'I expect you can smell the Puddingham-Piglets. They do have a bit of a pong. I think Georgie must wash his hair in chip fat.'

Archie needed to find a safe hiding place for the Smidgenfolk's not-stalagmite. It was far too big to fit in the box on the library mantelpiece. Perhaps he could put it in the greenhouse whilst he checked on the Spirit Oak? Maybe he could hide it under all the overgrown shrubs.

He grabbed a torch from the hall cupboard and wandered along to the door to the greenhouse. It was ajar. That was unusual. It was normally kept shut, to keep the heat in.

Tablet must have forgotten, Archie thought. The butler grew winter berries in pots in the greenhouse and would pop in to collect them occasionally. Archie shut the door behind him and found his way through the throng of plants to where the Spirit Oak had been planted. On his way the torchlight fell on a cluster of ferns growing by the path. Their long broad leaves were an ideal hiding place. Archie crouched by the ferns and lodged the conical stone in between their stalks so that it was hidden from view. As he got to his feet he came face to face with an unexpected visitor, lurking in the shadow of a nearby palm tree.

'I am here to warn you, boy,' said Audrey Buttereigh-Krumpitt, before he could speak. 'I know what you are trying to do and I am here to tell you to stop.'

'What are you talking about?' said Archie. 'How did you even get in here?'

She glared at him with her big, watery eyes.

'S.P.O.T.T.Y. came to your home to drum up support for the campaign. Whilst my colleagues distracted your mother, I slipped away to wait for you. Listen to me. You have no idea what you are dealing with. Give up your search for the key.'

The key! Audrey Buttereigh-Krumpitt knows about the key, thought Archie. There didn't seem much point pretending.

'It was you watching me through the window the other day!'

'We've been watching you for some time. Persons of power

are of interest to us. Especially persons who have a connection to the key. You are the Guardian of the Tree whose safe delivery was thanks to the Gate.'

'So why don't you want the key used again?' Archie asked. 'If we get the tunnel open, we can put the cable in there – without any workmen bothering your Yellow Beakytuft.'

'Tufted Yellowbeak! The workmen are of no consequence.'

That didn't sound like someone who cared about wildlife.

'No consequence? They're going to use dynamite to blow a hole from here to the coast! Not just a little tunnel. There won't be any Yeaky Tuftybell—'

'Tufted Yellowbeak—'

'Any … *birds* left at all!'

The woman smiled. 'It is of no matter. What matters is that you do not seek the key. I am forbidden to tell you why. This is not your affair, child. You have been warned.'

Ms Buttereigh-Krumpitt was swallowed up by the shadows.

'Wait!' Archie called. He heard the door open and close. The woman was gone.

'It's a good job she didn't see you hiding our summer

house under the ferns,' said a voice he recognised.

'Gafferty! Where are you?' Archie spun around. 'Did you follow me?'

'Behind you!' Gafferty giggled mischievously, as Archie turned again. 'Actually, I hooked myself on to your shirt. Stop spinning – I'm getting dizzy!'

The Smidgen-girl clambered up on to Archie's shoulder and detached her rope from his collar.

'I thought your dog would give the game away, sniffing around. He's seen us before, when we've visited the Hall. Tablet lends us a few things from the kitchen.'

'Is that why you're here?'

'No. I left my mum and dad a note so they know where I've gone. I wanted to see what you were up to with this key. It sounds like an adventure. Threatening people, plus dynamite – bring it on!'

'That's what Fliss would say.'

'Is she your girlfriend? I like the sound of her.'

'No!' Archie said hotly. 'The truth is, I don't really know what's going on. What have Audrey Buttereigh-Krumpitt and the S.P.O.T.T.Y. ladies got to do with the key? And why do they want to stop us from collecting all the pieces? And why don't they care about the dynamite? None of this makes sense!'

'Calm down,' said Gafferty, who had hopped on to a nearby tree branch as Archie paced the floor. 'I'm sure you'll work it out.'

Archie suddenly smiled.

'I may already have the answer to one question ...' he began.

Just then, there was a buzzing sound from one of the air vents that Blossom used to come and go from the greenhouse. The little honey dragon appeared, her tiny wings a blur of gold, and smoke snorted from her nose. She flew excited circles round Archie's head.

'Awake!' she growled. 'Awake! Awake!'

'At last!' said Archie. 'Everything is coming together.'

'What's it saying?' said Gafferty, staring at the dragon fearfully.

'The honey dragons,' said Archie. 'They've finally woken up!'

19

Although Archie wanted to go and see the dragons as soon as possible, and find out if they had the fourth part of Prang's key, it was now late in the evening. And anyway, he knew Fliss and Billy would be furious if he visited the Cavern of Honeystone without them. They were annoyed enough as it was when he gave them a full account of his evening, before classes began the next day.

'I can't believe you visited the Smidgenfolk, found the earth element to the key, had a strange encounter with Audrey Spotty-Krumpitt *and* received the news of the dragons waking up, all by yourself!' said Fliss, kicking a pebble across the schoolyard.

'Yesterday was a bit busy,' said Archie with a grin. 'But I wasn't alone. I think Gafferty Sprout could be a very useful ally, especially for what I've got in mind.'

'Can we trust her?' said Billy.

'Hello – I'm right here, you know!' Gafferty stuck her head out from Archie's schoolbag. 'Of course you can trust me!'

'Sorry,' said Billy. 'I've got a thing about spiders.'

'It's urban camouflage, nerd-boy. We make our clothes to look like things that people either ignore or avoid. Insects and spiders are a safe option. Plus they look cool.'

'Welcome, to the newest member of the Dundoodle Detectives!' said Fliss with a chuckle. 'Thank goodness there's another girl on the team. There's only so much stupid I can handle by myself.'

Gafferty managed to stay hidden for the rest of the school day, although she did occasionally slip away to explore the school. By the time the last lesson was over, Archie's bag was mysteriously full of paper, pencils and art supplies, and a satsuma from Mr Fingle's lunchbox.

'I'm teaching Gobkin his letters,' said Gafferty, by way of explanation. 'How am I supposed to do that without pens and paper? And Grub *loves* satsumas.'

Instead of going to Clootie Dumpling's as usual, Archie led the others into the maze of Dundoodle's

streets, which were busy with shoppers.

'Where are we going?' asked Fliss.

'S.P.O.T.T.Y. have been watching us,' said Archie. 'One of the ladies is behind us right now.'

Fliss glanced in a shop window. Sure enough, reflected in the glass was a familiar figure with slicked hair and a grey raincoat, keeping a little distance behind them.

'I'm going to try and lose her,' Archie continued. 'I want to be sure no one sees where we're going.'

'Why?' said Billy, as Archie suddenly changed course

and quickly ran down a narrow alley. The others hurried to catch up. 'You haven't told us what your plan is.'

'We're paying a visit to the S.P.O.T.T.Y. headquarters by the loch,' said Archie. 'Gafferty is going to do a little "borrowing" for us.'

There were more abrupt changes of course, diving in and out of shops and doubling back the way they'd come. Eventually, Archie felt comfortable that they had left the woman behind. Then – with Gafferty still in Archie's bag– the group made a dash for Fisherman's Way.

They kept to the shadows of the late afternoon, trying to stay out of sight, crouching in doorways or behind dustbins until they were sure no one was watching. Archie left the lane and took them along the pebble-covered shore of the loch, using the boathouses overhanging the beach as cover. The building supports hid them from anyone who might pass down the road.

'This is it,' whispered Billy, as they reached the shabby building that the campaign group had taken over. A light was on inside. The women were at home. 'Now please tell us why we're here!'

'S.P.O.T.T.Y. want us to stop looking for the elements of Prang's key,' said Archie. 'What better way to make sure we don't get our hands on them than to find them before us.'

'They've got some catching up to do. We've got two already, and we know where the third one is.'

'But it's all a waste of time if we don't have all four. I bet the key won't perform its unlocking spell unless we have the earth, air, fire and water elements together. They only need to get to one element first and the whole thing's spoilt.'

'The mystery magical woman who took the Breath of Maldemer from Gorm,' said Fliss. 'You think it's Audrey Buttereigh-Krumpitt!'

'Gorm said she was demanding and insistent,' said Billy. 'That could fit both her and Mrs Puddingham-Pye. But magical? Are the S.P.O.T.T.Y. ladies witches?'

'I don't know,' said Archie. 'I'm still not sure what's going on, but we need to open the tunnel and find *The Book of the Earth* before it's too late.'

'And what about her warning?' Gafferty piped up, peeping out from the cover of Archie's bag. 'She seemed pretty clear you shouldn't be opening that tunnel.'

'I know. But she also seemed clear that she's quite happy to let Mrs P-P and Gilbert Thaw deceive everyone into blowing up half the countryside instead, and lining their pockets in the process, and I'm not going to let that happen if I can help it.'

The others nodded.

'So I take it you want me to go in there and pinch the Breath of thingie?' said Gafferty. She climbed out of the bag. A Smidgen-rope was already attached to her belt and a tiny rucksack was on her back. 'I hope this Maldemer hadn't been eating garlic.'

'It's in some kind of flask,' Archie said. 'But don't do anything to put yourself in danger. We don't know exactly what these people are capable of.'

They tiptoed carefully up the stairs to the boathouse door, hoping that old and rickety didn't also mean squeaky and creaky. Gafferty – well practised at stealth – scrambled up the steps without a sound.

At the top of the stairs, they paused. Years of sun and rain (and more rain) had taken their toll on the door: it was warped and misshapen, so that a gap had formed between it and the floorboards. Gafferty gave the others a thumbs-up signal, then wriggled on her belly through the narrow space, looking very much like a spider. Archie listened at the door. He could hear footsteps of people inside the boathouse, but no voices. They could only hope that the arrival of the Smidgen-girl would go unnoticed …

'What have you to report?' Audrey Buttereigh-Krumpitt bellowed from inside the boathouse.

'There's some kind of meeting going on,' whispered Fliss. 'And I bet it's not about the Buffed Jellybeak.'

'Tufted Yellowbeak,' said Billy and Archie together.

'I followed the children, but lost them in the town,' one of the S.P.O.T.T.Y. ladies was saying. 'The children haven't gone to the dragons' cave. The Sisterhood have been patrolling the loch and there's been no sign of their boat. Perhaps your warning worked.'

'Perhaps,' Audrey Buttereigh-Krumpitt said. 'Though we can't be sure. The McBudge boy is stubborn, and as a wyrdworker he is dangerous. That's why we took the extra safeguard of claiming one of the key's four parts.

Still, if his wyrdie-abilities are developed, that may not be enough. But the Sisterhood of the Maelstrom cannot act as guardians of the key – that is not our job.'

'And what of the others – the adults?'

'When they don't find what they're looking for, they'll give up. That is our hope. Then the dark secret will be ours forever. Maintain the watch on the island. I will join you soon. By sunrise, we will have prevailed.'

There were footsteps. Someone was about to leave. Archie and the others scuttled down the stairs before anyone saw them. Billy, in his haste, stumbled, bumping into the back of Fliss. She missed her step, crashing to the ground and sending her schoolbag flying. It landed with a bump, spilling its contents over the lane. Before she could protest, Archie dragged Fliss into the shadow of the building, out of sight of the door. Billy joined them just as the door opened and Audrey's face appeared.

'What was that noise?' called the other woman from inside. The children held their breath.

'Cats, probably,' said Audrey. 'It looks like they've knocked over a litter bin.'

'They're always looking for fish scraps. They can't hunt fish for themselves like we do. By the way, have you seen my pen? I'm sure it was here a moment ago ...'

Audrey sniffed. 'You should be going,' she said, closing the door.

The children sighed with relief but stayed hidden, waiting for the other woman to leave, but she didn't appear in the lane. There were sounds from the back of the boathouse that faced on to the loch, where a wooden jetty ran out from the building for boats to moor.

'They must have a boat,' said Billy. 'But I don't see one.'

The woman walked along the jetty. She stopped at its end, then glanced around to make sure no one was watching. Her shape began to change, her arms and legs shrinking, and her grey oilskin raincoat began to stretch round her body, covering it tightly.

'What's happening to her?' said Fliss. 'She's being eaten by her clothes!'

'She's shape-shifting!' said Billy. 'Transforming into ... into ...'

'A seal!' said Archie. On the jetty lay a large grey creature with big eyes and shiny skin. It pushed itself off the platform and into the water, disappearing under its surface without causing a ripple.

'They're selkies!' gasped Billy. 'This Sisterhood of the Maelstrom must be made up of those legendary women who spend part of their lives as seals. Creepy Scale rating of six point two!'

'That's what was in the water when we were being chased by Saggie Aggie,' said Archie. 'We thought they were mermaids, but they were seals!'

'But they rescued us from Aggie,' said Fliss. 'If they don't want us finding the key, why didn't they just let Aggie catch us?'

'Another mystery to solve,' said Archie. 'Meanwhile, we've forgotten about Gafferty.'

The boys crept back up the staircase whilst Fliss quickly gathered up the belongings that had fallen from her bag. Archie risked a peek through the window. Audrey Buttereigh-Krumpitt had her back to him and was sitting at a table. She was scooping sardines from a tin on to a plate. Where was Gafferty?

There – an unusually large spider was slowly climbing down a wall. That was her! But what was she doing? Archie saw that she was making for a cupboard that had been pushed against the wall. On its surface was a tall, thin container with a lid that looked like it was made of silver. That must be the flask with the Breath of Maldemer! But how was Gafferty going to steal it? It was far too heavy for her – Archie hadn't thought of that!

In the lane, Fliss was studying some little bits of paper in her hand. 'Archie,' she hissed. 'I think I've found something important.'

'Hang on,' he replied. 'Gafferty might need our help.' He and Billy watched as the spider quietly landed on the cupboard.

'The flask is bigger than her,' said Billy. 'She'll never be able to pick it up.'

But Gafferty didn't try to lift the flask. Instead she leaned against it and, keeping one eye on Audrey, slowly began pushing it towards the edge of the cupboard.

'It'll hit the ground and make a huge noise,' said Billy. 'She'll be found out!'

'No,' said Archie with a grin. 'See that pile of fishing nets, next to the cupboard? They'll catch the flask. It won't make a sound!'

At that moment, Audrey looked up from her sardines and sniffed the air. She looked around. Gafferty swiftly dived behind the flask, and the boys ducked down below the window sill. They heard Audrey get up from her chair and move about. Archie peered over the window sill. He gasped.

'She's going to the cupboard!' he squeaked. Gafferty crouched behind the flask, trying to look as spidery as possible. Audrey paused to study the silver object.

Has she noticed it's moved? Archie wondered. His heart was in his mouth as Audrey's hand reached out. *It's all over*, he thought.

Then she opened the cupboard door and pulled out a bottle of ketchup. She took it back to the table and sat down, squirting tomato sauce over the fish. She began to eat messily, oil running down her whiskery chin. Archie slumped next to Billy.

'That was close!'

They watched as Gafferty managed to tip the flask over the edge of the cupboard. It landed softly in the net, then the Smidgen-girl clambered down into the netting with it. She was able to drag the flask through the gaps in the net so that it lay on its side on the floorboards.

Gafferty jumped nimbly on to the container, rolling it along the floor using her feet, like a circus acrobat. She steered it towards the door. Archie reached for the handle, carefully opening the door just enough to drag the flask and girl through. Then they dashed back down the stairs, Gafferty clinging on to Archie's bag. Fliss was waiting in the lane.

'We did it!' said Archie, running up to her. 'Or at least, Gafferty did.'

Fliss's face was pale. She didn't look happy.

'I might have made a discovery,' she said. 'And it's bad. Very bad.'

21

'Tell us on the way back to the Hall,' said Archie. It wasn't often that Fliss looked worried. 'We need to get out of here before Audrey discovers someone's taken her Breath away. Literally.'

They ran up Fisherman's Way back to the centre of Dundoodle. Once they'd taken the turning that led to Honeystone Hall, Fliss explained.

'When I was pushed over,' she glared at Billy, 'all my stuff fell out of my bag, including the pieces of Gilbert Thaw's business card.'

'The one you tore up yesterday,' said Archie, nodding.

'As the pieces were mixed up, all the letters were mixed up with them. It was like one of those puzzles where you're given a muddle of letters and have to work out the words they spell.'

'You already know the words they spell,' said Billy. 'Gilbert Thaw.'

'No,' said Fliss. 'I saw something else.' She stopped and took out a notebook and pen. First she wrote Gilbert's name on a blank page:

GILBERT THAW.

Underneath, she wrote another word, crossing out each letter she used from the engineer's name. She showed it to the others:

WATERBLIGHT.

'Where have I heard that before?' said Archie.

'Waterblight the Giant-smith!' said Billy. 'Ghostly Gorm mentioned him – he was the evil warlock who built the giants, in the war against the gods! Do you think Gilbert is Waterblight?'

'It has to be,' said Fliss. 'It's too much of a coincidence. Though he must be hundreds – if not thousands – of years old by now, like Aggie. And he's just the sort of person who would make a deal with Mrs Puddingham-Pye.'

'That's so clever, Fliss,' said Archie, rubbing his chin. 'We'd never have known otherwise. Suddenly things are starting to get a little clearer.'

They hurried back to the Hall.

'We've got to get to Pookiecrag Island and see the honey dragons right away!' said Archie. 'The dynamite is set to go off tonight – we've no time to lose.'

'What about S.P.O.T.T.Y.?' said Gafferty. 'Or this Sisterhood, as they're calling themselves. They said they were patrolling the loch. They'll try and stop us.'

Archie smiled. 'I might have a plan for that. I know what I want my Spirit Oak to be. I only hope it's been doing a bit of growing since I last saw it.'

They ran straight to the greenhouse, meeting Sherbet along the way. He had a nose for adventure and knew something was up. Archie led them to the clump of ferns under which he'd hidden the Smidgenfolk's stone summer house and put it in his bag with the flask. Then he took them to where the Spirit Oak grew. It was very different from the seedling they had planted in the flower bed a few days before.

'If it weren't for the leaves growing out of it, I don't think I'd know that was a tree at all,' said Fliss. 'It's more like a tea tray!'

It was an odd-looking plant. The trunk had grown broad, flat and shaped like a knight's shield, its surface smooth to the touch. A few tufts of greenery sprouted from it, but there were no branches or twigs to speak of.

'It's almost perfect,' said Archie. 'The Spirit Oak did know what I needed. Now for a few finishing touches ...'

He pointed his fingers at the young tree and concentrated. It might have been his closeness to the earth element of Prang's key, or just that Archie had grown into his wyrdworking powers, but the magic flowed through him more easily than before.

The Spirit Oak's trunk began to stretch and curve slightly under his guidance. The leaves fell softly to the ground. Archie stepped forward and gently picked the finished object out of the flower bed. It was light in weight and felt cool to the touch. There was still a wonky bit on one side, a scar from the accident that didn't want to heal, but overall it looked finished, whatever it might be.

'Congratulations,' said Billy, a puzzled frown on his forehead. 'You've made an ironing board. What are you going to do – give Gilbert's overalls a press?'

Archie laughed. 'Not quite. Come on, let's get to the boat. You'll see what this does soon.'

He tucked the piece of wood under his arm and led them to the library. There, he took the bottle of silver-water from the box on the mantelpiece and added it to the other things in his bag. Fliss opened the secret door in the bookcase and the children scurried down the hidden passage to the cave where Archie's magical boat waited.

'If Gilbert is a warlock,' said Fliss, as they clambered into the boat, which appeared to have transformed back to its original form since their underwater adventure, 'why does he want to help Mrs Puddingham-Pye make a big hole in the ground? He can't be interested in roads and electrical cables and making money, can he?'

'Audrey said something about a "dark secret",' said Billy. 'Is he after that, do you think?'

'Maybe he's after *The Book of the Earth*,' said Archie. 'Perhaps he found out about it somehow. I think Waterblight's tried to get the pieces of Prang's key in the past. Did you see the scar on his arm? They were teeth marks – like the teeth of a shark. I think he visited Aggie as well, but only just avoided becoming dinner.'

'He's a warlock – what about his magic powers?' said Gafferty. She'd never been in a boat before and watched with keen interest as it slowly launched itself away from the shore.

'He might have been able to beat Aggie once, long ago,' said Billy. 'But Gorm said most of the warlocks' magic was taken from them by the gods. Waterblight must be operating on reduced power now.'

'So maybe he's given up using magic to open the tunnel,' said Archie, 'and he's going to use brute force instead, then claim *The Book of the Earth* and take its magic for himself. That's what I'd do.'

Fliss shot a look of disapproval at him.

'Be careful, Archie,' she said. 'You're sounding very Puddingham-Pyeish! And, speaking of Mrs P-P, what's her involvement in all this? Maybe she does know about *The Book of the Earth* after all, and the twins were just good at lying?'

Archie was silent. Fliss was right, things still didn't make sense. They were missing something. And she was right about him sounding Puddingham-Pyeish. Had he guessed correctly about Waterblight's plan, or was he judging the warlock by his own standards, his own desires? The power contained in the Book was such a temptation – what would Archie be prepared to do to get it?

The sun was low in the pink-tinged sky as the boat sped across the loch, its destination the island of Pookiecrag, where the ruins of the old McBudge castle stood. The water was calm and the fresh spring air should have made the journey quite pleasant. But the boat began to pitch, its sides shuddering, as if it were riding over unseen obstacles.

'What's going on?' said Billy.

Dark shapes rose from the depths of the water, following the boat and swimming alongside it, easily keeping pace with the magical craft. Sherbet barked a warning as one of them threw themselves against the boat, its body buffeting the side and knocking it off course.

A grey head broke the surface, its gentle face radiating anger. There was no mistaking them for mermaids this time. The Sisterhood of the Maelstrom were following their orders.

'The selkies!' cried Billy. 'They've come for us!'

22

The seals bombarded them from all angles, pushing the boat roughly in one direction then another. With each hit, its passengers were rocked violently and splashed with icy-cold spray. After a particularly heavy blow, Gafferty only just escaped being flung into the water. Sherbet barked furiously at the troublemakers.

The boat battled on defiantly, but its progress was slow.

'It can't take much more of this,' yelled Fliss. 'We're not even halfway across the loch. We'll be swamped with water if they keep hitting us.'

'*I* can't take any more of this!' whimpered Billy. 'Is it possible to be seasick when you're not even at sea?'

Archie picked up the piece of Spirit Oak wood.

'It's time to put the brothers' gift into action,' he said. 'If the selkies see me leaving, maybe they'll stop attacking the boat.'

'You're abandoning ship?' said Billy, horrified. 'How?'

Archie laid the piece of wood across the boat so that it rested on the boat's sides. He clambered on top of it, slinging his bag on his back.

'I'll only be gone for a bit. And if this works like I want it to, I'll have made an alternative magical transport, better than any witch's broom!'

'So it's a surfboard!' said Fliss, watching in astonishment as he attempted to keep his balance.

'I was thinking more of a hoverboard,' Archie said nervously. 'That's if I can control it!'

'Archie, either you're completely bonkers or you're going to be the coolest wizardy wyrdworker person in the whole of Dundoodle! Possibly both.'

'When I've gone, make the boat head back to Dundoodle, as if you're going home. The selkies should back off then. But go to the Prangstone instead – I'll meet you there.'

'I'm coming with you,' said Gafferty, jumping on to the board and grabbing Archie's ankle. 'I've always wanted to see the honey dragons' cave. I'm not missing out because of a bunch of grouchy, watery bullies.'

Archie concentrated. He'd done this before, but last time it was a coffin that he'd used as a vehicle! This should be easier – there was a connection between him and the Spirit Oak. They could sense each other. The board wobbled, then pushed off at high speed from the boat.

Gafferty screamed as it smashed straight into the loch, bouncing along the surface of the water like a flat pebble thrown hard. It was the wonky bit of the board, Archie realised, that made the craft unbalanced. He focused his thoughts and with a mighty effort and one final wobble, they soared skyward. Gafferty screamed again.

'Sorry for the rough take-off,' said Archie. He made the wyrdie-board circle upwards before setting it towards Pookiecrag Castle. Gafferty gingerly leaned over the edge.

'You were right!' she said. 'The Sisterhood are leaving the boat alone.'

The selkies seemed confused. Some were swimming round in circles, uncertain of what to do next, whilst others bobbed in the water, watching Archie's escape. The boat with Billy, Fliss and Sherbet was already on its way back towards the town.

The hoverboard made short work of the journey to the island. Archie brought it softly in to land in the roofless great hall of the ancient ruins.

'I hope the honey dragons had a good sleep over the winter,' he said, climbing off the board and propping it up against the old fireplace. 'I wouldn't want to be the person who bothers a tired fire-breathing monster.'

The entrance to the Cavern of Honeystone was hidden behind a trapdoor in the fireplace. Archie opened it and ran as fast as he could down the long tunnel that led right into the heart of Ben Doodle mountain. Gafferty clung tightly to the strap of his schoolbag, slightly terrified by the thought of seeing so many enormous (at least, to her) dragons.

The sight of the cavern made her eyes almost pop out of her head: it was filled with clusters of huge golden honeystone crystals, made by the dragons with their magical fire using nectar from flowers. They arrived to find the friendly creatures munching on the delicious honeystone, recharging themselves after their long nap. There too was Blossom – she'd missed her dragon family and had been getting reacquainted.

'Jings is expecting you,' she said, pointing to the centre of the cavern.

'Old Jings is the oldest dragon,' Archie told Gafferty, as he trod a careful path through the glittering honeystone forest. 'If anyone knows about the final element of Prang's key, it will be him.'

They found the ancient dragon in his nest of crystals, gnawing on a chunk of honeystone as best as he was able, since he lacked a few teeth.

'The young dragon tells me you're in need of something,' Jings said, eyeing Archie steadily. 'The honey dragons are ready to aid the McBudges, as always.'

'Thank you,' said Archie, feeling nervous under the creature's gaze. 'We've been searching for the elements to the key of Prang the Pebble-dashed, the troll captain whose ship brought the Wyrdie Tree to the old forest. I have them all here, except one.' He patted his school-bag.

'That was before even my time,' said Jings. 'Though I've heard the tale.'

'An inscription we found said *dare the cave of the fiery*

lizards, so I came here. Do you know what the final element of the key is?'

'I do. The knowledge has been passed down from one chief dragon to the next.'

'Unlike the Smidgenfolk,' muttered Gafferty. 'We love to chat about the weather, but things like ancient magical troll-keys – forget it!'

'But the war between the gods and the giants left many scars. Deep scars,' continued Jings. 'If you seek to use the key, you may reopen old wounds from that time. Think hard, young McBudge. All actions have consequences, so you must consider your decisions as best as you can. There may be no time for regrets.'

Archie was uneasy. This felt like a warning. Fliss had always been unsure about this adventure; she called it 'meddling'. But he was the Guardian of the Wyrdie Tree, a wyrdworker – surely that meant he could handle this? And he wanted *The Book of the Earth* so much!

'I understand,' he said. 'Will you give me the final element of the key?'

Old Jings sighed smokily and looked him straight in the eye.

'No,' the dragon said.

23

Archie stood open-mouthed. Had he heard right? Old Jings knew about the key and knew Archie as a friend – why was he refusing to help?

'You said you were ready to aid the McBudges,' he stammered, 'but now you're saying you won't. I can't fail now that I've got this far!' He paced before the dragon, panic rising inside him. 'Is it some kind of treasure? A magical object?' He picked up a piece of honeystone that was lying on the floor. 'Is it honeystone? That has magical powers. Please tell me – we're running out of time!'

'Calm yourself,' commanded Old Jings. He was old and frail, but he was still a dragon. 'It is far simpler than that. It is not a trinket, or a jewel, but a living thing – the fire from a dragon. That is our element of the key.

'I will not give you my fire, for I fear what may be behind the door that this key unlocks. Prang the troll would not speak of it. But another dragon might help you.'

That was enough for Archie. He ran back towards the cavern's entrance.

'I can't believe we had the last element under our noses all along!' he said.

'It was a good job the Sisterhood didn't know you had a dragon living in your greenhouse,' said Gafferty, resolutely hanging on to his bag strap, 'or Blossom could have been in trouble. But, Archie, about what the old dragon said ... Do you really want to go through with this?'

'If we don't get inside that tunnel then Mrs Puddingham-Pye and Waterblight the Warlock will,' said Archie firmly. 'And they'll have their hands on *The Book of the Earth*. I'm pretty sure they won't be using it for the benefit of mankind – or Smidgenkind, for that matter. The only way to stop them is to get there first.'

Blossom was still where they'd left her. She looked at Archie quizzically.

'Blossom, we need your help,' Archie began. 'Your Dragon-fire, to be precise. Jings has said he won't help us – and that's his choice – so you're our only hope. Please come with us. Please help us.'

The dragon studied their faces, seeming to consider the issue. Then she sighed and rolled her eyes. 'Completely bonkers!' she growled. 'Let's go!'

The sun was setting when they took off from the castle, Archie and Gafferty sailing through the air on the wyrdie-board and the little dragon flying beside them. The loch was a sheet of dark glass below them. There was no sign of the selkies anywhere.

'We should make it to the Prangstone in time,' said Archie. 'Before the explosion is set off.'

'Do you know how to make the key work?' said Gafferty.

'Not exactly. In fact, not at all. There wasn't a manual. We're just going to have to see what happens.'

They reached Dundoodle, and followed the line of Fisherman's Way along the loch. The boathouse windows were dark. Had the Sisterhood noticed the Breath of Maldemer was missing? Archie could just make out the boat a little offshore – Billy and Fliss had made it! Sherbet barked and wagged his tail as the board alighted on the water beside them.

'You've been ages,' said Fliss. 'We were getting worried.'

'So was I,' Archie admitted, 'but Blossom has come to

help – the last element is Dragon-fire! It's time to put them together.'

'How?' said Billy.

'The cone-thing looks like it's meant to hold something,' said Fliss. 'Perhaps you put the other things in it?'

Archie nodded. He knelt on the hoverboard and opened his bag. First he took out the Smidgenfolk's summer house.

'This is for earth,' he said, holding it up. Then he took out the bottle of silver-water. He removed the stopper and poured the strange liquid into the stone's cone-shaped hollow.

'This is for water.'

Rather than pooling in the bottom of the cone, the liquid crawled up and over the sides, spilling into and filling the engraved patterns so that it looked like the stone had been inlaid with shiny metal.

Fliss unscrewed the flask containing the Breath of Maldemer and handed it to Archie. He upturned the flask over the cone.

'This is for air.'

A rushing breeze swept from the mouth of the flask and formed a spinning ball over the cone. Archie turned to Blossom. She blew a stream of golden fire into the ball of air.

'This is for fire.'

The Dragon-fire was captured inside the ball of air and turned blue, a sure sign of magic.

Archie held the key up so that it lit their faces and gave the water beneath them an icy brilliance.

'It's like a magical Olympic torch,' said Fliss. 'So beautiful! I wish my front door key looked like that!'

'A torch – of course!' said Archie. 'A light to guide you through the darkness of the tunnel.'

The key began to quake in Archie's hand.

THE MOMENT OF MY FREEDOM HAS ARRIVED.

The voice – Archie had almost forgotten it in the hurry to find the key! He winced as it echoed through his mind. It was close!

I WILL COMPLETE THE TASK FOR WHICH I WAS MADE. I WILL DESTROY!

All at once, several heads emerged from the loch around them.

'The selkies!' said Billy.

'Foolish children!' hissed one of the creatures, staring at the key. 'What have you done?'

There came a shout from the shore. Mrs Puddingham-Pye and Gilbert Thaw were clambering across the cliff towards the Prangstone, followed by Gilbert's workmen. Mrs P-P carried her broom and had a snarling Garstigan sitting on her shoulder. Thaw was no longer in his overalls and was dressed in a long black robe. He looked very much like a wicked sorcerer and stared wildly at the key, which trembled in Archie's hand.

'Gilbert *is* Waterblight!' said Fliss. 'But what are they doing here?'

'It must be where they planned to set off the explosion,' said Billy.

'This isn't good,' said Archie. 'They weren't supposed to be here!'

It was too late. The key was shaking and blue light began to erupt from the churning ball of air, firing in all directions. The key flew out of Archie's hand and struck the Prangstone, its pointed end burying itself into the rock.

The dazzling rays continued to pour from it, and they

began to swirl and rotate, spinning faster and faster. A huge circle of light formed in the air in front of them. But it wasn't flat – it was as if a hole had opened in the sky and they could see through to a dark, dark place inside, darker than the night sky around it.

'What's happening?' said Archie. 'Where's the tunnel?'

'There's no tunnel,' screeched the selkie. 'There never was! Only we knew the truth, Prang told us – the Gate is a dimensional portal, a shortcut through time and space, opened by Maldemer! We know it as the Maelstrom. No ship has ever passed through these mountains. It was teleported from one side to the other! But not only is the Gate a portal – it is also a prison.'

At that moment, a giant, craggy hand appeared through the hole in the sky, reaching for the outside world. 'FINALLY. I AM FREE.'

24

The hand was followed by an enormous arm, then another hand. Something was pulling itself out of the portal and into their world! They watched in horrified fascination as a massive head appeared, cracked and weathered like the summit of a mountain, its eyes burning with hatred.

Archie was frozen, his hand still shaking from when he had held the key.

What have I done? he thought over and over. *They were never after* The Book of the Earth *– that was just me! They wanted this … thing!*

'Creepy Scale rating of … of …' Billy began, his eyes as wide as saucers. He paused. 'I think we can all agree this one is completely off the scale!'

Mrs Puddingham-Pye looked on gleefully, as Waterblight called out to the monster.

'Magog, my child,' he said. 'My creation! I have brought you back into the world after so many years of imprisonment!'

The man waded into the loch, his hands held up as if he wanted to hug the monster.

'If only I'd known earlier what had happened to you! My ship followed you across the sea, but it was attacked by Maldemer's water dragons. By the time we had escaped them, you had disappeared. I thought you were destroyed! But finally you called for me, after so many long years, and I rejoiced! With my brother warlocks all gone, I had thought I was alone.'

He shook a fist at the air and his voice became menacing.

'Now, together, we can rule these pitiful mortals, as we were destined to do! Everything will be better – it will all be as it should be – a warlock in charge and humanity at my feet.'

The giant heaved itself out of the Gate, sending waves over the loch as it finally planted its feet in the water. The children clung on to the boat as it fought the force of the surf. The monster towered over them, turning its head to look at a world it had not set foot in for thousands of years. The giant growled, then spoke with the voice already familiar to Archie.

'TIME HAS PASSED AND I HAVE BEEN FORGOTTEN. BUT SOON ALL SHALL KNOW ME.'

'Magog, to me!' Waterblight ordered, a look of triumph and delight on his face. 'Come and serve your master!'

Magog stooped, its fiery gaze falling upon the warlock. Then it reached out its hand and picked Waterblight off the ground.

'What are you doing? Magog – release me!'

'PATHETIC LITTLE SORCEROR. YOU DID NOT RELEASE ME. IT TOOK A CHILD TO DO WHAT YOU HAVE SPENT YEARS TRYING AND FAILING TO DO. YOUR MAGIC HAS FADED. I WILL SERVE YOU NO MORE.'

Waterblight screamed in fear. The workmen sprang towards the giant, jumping into the loch and punching and tearing at Magog's huge legs in an attempt to rescue the man. Magog kicked them away, the force throwing them against the cliff face, where their bodies smashed into pieces, like broken flowerpots.

'Golems!' said Billy, as the others gasped in shock.

'The workmen were golems – magical robots made of clay. Creepy Scale rating of seven. Waterblight must have spent what power he had left to create them and use them as his servants.'

'NOW, WARLOCK, YOU WILL SUFFER WHAT I ENDURED.'

As if he were nothing more than an unwanted toy, Waterblight was thrown through the Gate, his arms and legs flailing helplessly, and into the blackness beyond. They heard a final shriek before the portal shrank away to nothing. The key's light failed. It tumbled out of the Prangstone, dropped into the water below and sank out of sight. Archie collapsed on to his hoverboard, covered in sweat.

'The Book!' he cried. '*The Book of the Earth*. I'll – we'll never get it now!'

The giant turned its massive head towards Archie, examining him almost curiously.

'THE BOOK IS NO MORE. I LAY DORMANT IN THE DARKNESS FOR CENTURIES BEFORE THE BOOK CAME TO ME. I SENSED ITS POWER AND CONSUMED IT. ITS POWER BECAME MINE.

'IT LIT A FIRE IN MY HEAD – THOUGHTS I HAD NOT KNOWN BEFORE. THAT IS HOW I EVOLVED

BEYOND A WARLOCK'S PLAYTHING. I CALLED OUT TO HIM FOR HELP, BUT I HAD PLANS OF MY OWN. I BECAME MY OWN MASTER.'

The Book of the Earth had been destroyed! Archie couldn't believe it – everything they'd worked for, spent so much time on, had ended in disaster!

'I WILL FINISH THE TASK I WAS SET,' Magog bellowed. 'THOUGH NOT BECAUSE I AM COMMANDED, BUT BECAUSE I DESIRE IT. THE OFFSPRING OF THE WORLD TREE SHALL BE UPROOTED. THEN I SHALL BE UNCHALLENGED.'

He slowly turned and began moving through the water.

'He's going to destroy the Wyrdie Tree!' said Billy. 'I didn't think this could get any worse, but it has, and rather spectacularly.'

'Archie, we have to do something!' said Fliss.

Archie didn't answer. He knelt, in a daze.

She leaned over the side of the boat and shook him. 'Archie, we need to fix this.'

'Yes,' he said, miserably. 'But this is my fault. You were right – I was meddling. I was greedy. I'm the reason this has happened. I'll fix it.'

'No,' said Fliss, firmly. 'We helped you, and we'll help

you sort it out. You know we will! But we need to do something soon. If Magog destroys the Tree then you won't have any powers, and without your magic we won't last much longer than those golems.'

'We will help too,' growled the selkie. The other seals had gathered round the boat. 'The Sisterhood of the Maelstrom was charged with guarding the Gate and we have failed in that duty. We are creatures of water magic – combined with your earth magic, we might make a stand against the giant. But the girl is right. We must act now.'

There was a cruel laugh from overhead. Above, Mrs Puddingham-Pye sat on her broomstick. Garstigan was curled up on its end like some hideous, hissing cat.

'Quite the achievement, Urchin,' she said. 'Without your interference, Magog would never be free!'

Archie could do nothing but look miserable.

'You're so out of your depth, boy,' the woman continued. 'I knew this would happen – your inexperience would get the better of you. A silly, overconfident little child. You were never up to the job of being Guardian. It should have been me!'

'And what kind of mess would we be in if you *were* the Guardian?' snapped Fliss. 'Worse than this, that's for sure!'

'Worse, but much more tastefully refined and glamorous,' Garstigan said helpfully, before being silenced by a look from the witch.

'Why don't you help, if you're so good at this?' called out Gafferty. 'Make yourself useful instead of flying around like an overgrown bat.'

'Help?' said Mrs Puddingham-Pye. 'Help? Why on earth would I do that? I wanted Magog released. Waterblight was an old fool and the giant has saved me the bother of getting rid of him myself. I'll find a way of controlling Magog and then I'll be the one in charge.'

'He seems pretty independently minded to me!' said Billy. 'And if he destroys the Wyrdie Tree, he'll destroy all the magic in Dundoodle – including yours.'

'I've studied magic – I've taken it from many sources, not only the Tree. And Magog will need a guide in this new world. I shall make myself useful to him, and in return he shall be useful to me.'

She flew high into the air with a cackle, trailing after the giant. Magog strode heavily through the water, passing the unsuspecting town and blocking out its twinkling lights as he moved.

Archie got to his feet, filled with determination. Mrs Puddingham-Pye's mockery was the last straw. Yes, if they worked together they could fix it. He was the Guardian of the Tree, and it needed him – he mustn't give up.

'We need to get to Pookiecrag Castle,' he said, thinking quickly. 'The giant is strong, but he's slow. We can easily get there before he's halfway to the old forest. Once we're there, I have an idea that might stop him.'

'What are we going to do?' said Gafferty.

'We're going to fight the giant with one of our own.'

25

They set off at once – Archie and Gafferty on the wyrdie-board, skimming across the water, with Fliss, Billy and Sherbet following in the boat. Blossom flew overhead, whilst the selkies swam below. A full moon lit their way, its pale radiance adding a ghostly tinge to their grim faces.

'What was Magog doing inside the portal-dimensional-doodah-thingy?' asked Gafferty. 'I thought the giants were long gone.'

'They are,' said the lead selkie, who was presumably Audrey Buttereigh-Krumpitt the rest of the time. 'Magog was the giant who chased the troll ship across the sea to stop the Wyrdie Tree from being planted.

'The Gate was opened to allow it to escape him. Most thought that he was left behind in the sea and had given up the chase. Waterblight thought him destroyed. But Prang knew that Magog had followed the ship into the portal. When Prang locked the Gate, the giant was trapped inside, and he's been there ever since.'

'Then Prang split the key and gave the parts to the magical folk,' said Archie.

'He offered the key to us,' said the seal. 'But we felt its burden was too heavy and it should be divided. We promised to keep watch on the key's guardians, who knew nothing of the Gate's secret. No one would know, in case they should be tempted to release the giant held within it. We swore to keep the secret forever.'

Archie shivered. He had been tempted to open the Gate, though by the power of the Book rather than the giant.

'No wonder you didn't care if Waterblight blew up the mountains,' he said. 'It wouldn't make any difference to the Gate. He didn't know about its existence either. He thought Magog was inside a tunnel.'

'The aim of our campaign was to deceive and frustrate Waterblight. If we opposed the construction work, it would slow him down – waste his time and his resources. He was old, his powers mostly gone. He was unable to do much more than create toys, like the golems, and he was reliant on the witch for help. If he guessed we were magical folk trying to stop him blowing up the mountain, we hoped he would simply think he was on the right track and continue in his pointless mission.'

'Because you knew the only way to release Magog was with the key.'

'Waterblight found out about the key from the Prangstone inscription. But he gave up on the hunt for it after Aggie humiliated him. That's when he came up with idea of the electric cable and recruited the witch to his cause. Maybe he would have given up again, once the explosion failed to give him what he wanted, or he would continue his search somewhere else – that was our hope.'

'But he knew Magog *was* there, as he could talk to him. I could hear them talking – or at least, I could hear Magog, though I couldn't sense any magic.'

'Magog was there – in the same place, but in a different dimension, separate from our own. That barrier stopped you from sensing the magic properly. We hadn't counted on Magog becoming independent of thought and calling out to the warlock. It could have ruined our plans.'

'And your powers are still growing, Archie,' said Billy, who had been writing the conversation down as best he could in the moonlight. 'Magog and Waterblight have been communicating for some years, but you've only picked up on it recently. With more time perhaps you could have sensed what was really going on.'

Archie sighed. It was another reminder of his inexperience, although he knew Billy didn't mean it that way.

They reached Pookiecrag Island. The boat moored at the jetty.

'I've never been so glad to get on to dry land,' said Billy as he clambered out. 'Sailing's no fun when the loch's as busy as this!'

The selkies became human once more. They stood round Archie expectantly.

'Where are we going to get a giant from?' said Fliss. 'You can't hire them, as far as I know.'

'But you can make them,' said Archie. 'Like Waterblight did. Remember how Gorm said giants were built and quarried – constructed? We're going to do just that, with a bit of help.'

'Using what?' said Billy. 'We don't have a quarry.'

Fliss's eyes shone with excitement as she realised what Archie meant.

'We don't have a quarry,' she said, looking around, 'but we do have plenty of building material! Archie, you're a completely bonkers genius.'

'You're going to make it out of the ruins of Pookiecrag Castle?' said Gafferty. 'This I have to see!'

'I always thought this place looked like the bones of an old giant,' said Billy.

'Now it's going to be the bones of a new one,' Archie said. 'I only hope I've the strength to make it happen. The castle was a McBudge castle – I've a connection to it, so I hope it'll work for me.'

'We will help,' said Audrey gently. 'Concentrate. Call upon the Tree.'

Archie took a deep breath. He shut his eyes. The others watched as roots suddenly emerged from the ground, winding amongst the rubble of the castle, picking up stones as they moved, rearranging them and knitting them together.

As the castle shrank, a shape slowly grew. Bit by bit – first feet, then legs, then body – a huge stone figure began to form.

'That's it, Archie!' said Fliss. 'It's working!'

'Keep going,' said Gafferty.

Glancing back over the loch, they could all see Magog was getting closer and closer to the forest, his eyes spots of angry red light in the darkness. But they couldn't disturb Archie. They couldn't risk him losing focus.

After a painful few minutes, the new giant finally stood before them.

'It has a ... certain style,' said Billy.

It was a bit wonky and odd-looking, Archie had to admit. It had a doorway in one arm, a chimney on its shoulder and an old bird's nest on its head. Roots and vines ran through it like veins. But for a first attempt it wasn't bad.

'It is the turn of the Sisterhood now,' said Audrey. 'We will put some flesh on this skeleton.'

The women raised their arms towards the loch. A huge column of water rose out of it, snaking towards the motionless giant. The conjured water enveloped the stones, forming a smooth, glassy body round the rough, weatherworn rock.

'We'll call him Pookiecrag,' said Archie.

'I can see fish swimming in his head!' said Gafferty.

'Now, join hands!' said Audrey. 'We must work together to control this thing, or its power may prove too much for us.'

Archie and the women linked hands. Slowly, steadily, the creature moved, testing its joints, flexing its limbs and studying its surroundings.

Flying above the trees, Blossom had been watching

Magog's progress across the loch. She landed on Fliss's shoulder, muttering.

'I'm afraid there's no time for a test drive,' Fliss called over to them. 'Pookiecrag needs to go into action!'

Without hesitating, Pookiecrag marched into the loch, wading quickly towards Magog.

The other giant soon noticed the newcomer and halted, uncertain if it faced a friend or a foe. As Pookiecrag advanced, Magog decided. He would stand no rivals.

The monsters faced each other … and charged!

26

The two giants collided in an explosion of water and rock, dust and foam. It was difficult to see where one giant began and the other ended. Magog roared with fury as the two wrestled and fought, the moonlit loch churning around them.

Fist pounded against chest, and fingers of stone gouged into arms of granite, sending firefly-like sparks diving into the lake to hiss and spit and smoke.

Archie could feel each blow from Magog vibrate through his mind and into his body, could feel how evenly matched the two giants were.

Come on, Pookiecrag. You can do it – you have to!

There was something else too, small but noticeable: a thought that was not his own. Savage, confused and hot with raw emotion. Pookiecrag was aware of himself, and Archie could feel the young giant's untamed mind resisting his control, an instinct to destroy threatening to overwhelm the need to stay disciplined. Audrey was right, they would have to work hard to keep the creature restrained.

'This is what it must have been like in the war with the gods,' said Billy, glancing from the battle over to where Archie stood with the selkie women, their faces lost in concentration.

'I can hardly look!' said Gafferty.

'I hope Archie will be all right,' was all Fliss could say, as she cuddled Sherbet.

Magog was gaining the upper hand. The older giant made a grab for Pookiecrag's head and locked him in a chokehold. Magog's anger fuelled him and gave him a speed and ferocity that was terrifying to see. He began to force Pookiecrag on to his knees.

Archie could sense panic in Pookiecrag's mind. *Keep calm*, he thought. *That's your weapon. Magog's anger makes him wild, frenzied and wilful. He's not focused – use it to your advantage!*

It wasn't working. They were losing the connection with Pookiecrag. His head was filled with chaos and fear.

Magog pushed the younger giant down into the loch. His foot was on Pookiecrag's back, shoving him into the water and stopping him from getting to his feet.

Pookiecrag floundered in the crashing waves. Magog was going to win!

'I've got to help!' said Archie. He let go of Audrey's hand and grabbed his schoolbag, taking out the rejected sweets.

'What are you doing?' said Billy. 'You can't seriously be hungry?'

'I just need a little extra bit of McBudge firepower,' said Archie. 'Extra extra extra extra strong firepower!'

He picked out the mints that Mr Fairbairn had thought were a safety hazard and waved at Magog.

'Your time is over, Magog!' Archie called, jumping on to the wyrdie-board and sailing into the air around the combatants. 'Your old magic cannot win against the new. You belong in the past, to a different world. You will be defeated!'

The ancient giant glowered at Archie as the board circled his massive head.

'NEVER!' he roared, almost knocking the boy off his feet and into the loch.

But the distraction had worked. Magog's grip relaxed

and Pookiecrag was able to raise his head – his huge, watery mouth open in a silent appeal. Archie guided the board sharply downwards and hurled the sweets straight at it as he flew past. His aim was good. The sweets tumbled into Pookiecrag's cavernous throat.

Archie landed back on the island with a bump and joined hands with Audrey again. They watched the mints fizz and froth inside the see-through monster. It twitched and ice formed on the surface of its skin. Then, throwing its head back, Pookiecrag let out a roar that sent a blast of bitterly cold air howling across the lake.

With a glowing white rage in his eyes, Pookiecrag slammed his shoulder into Magog's chest, breaking the older giant's grip. His frosted, glassy skin buffered his enemy's blows, his water–earth magic greater in strength now, with a spark of extra extra extra extra strong firepower burning inside.

Archie whooped in triumph. He knew, as he battled

Magog in his mind, that deep down it was his connection to the stones of the castle, his family's old home, that made the difference. The castle was part of him, so he was part of the giant. He was fighting Magog and he was going to win.

Pookiecrag landed a blow to Magog's face, causing the older giant to stagger backwards, stunned. Archie saw his chance, and Pookiecrag drew back his mighty fist.

Before Magog had time to react, he was hit by the full force of a punch to his chest. It drove a crater into the monster's body, cracks travelling in all directions through his arms, legs and head. Magog tried to cry out, but his face began to shatter and his body began to splinter into dust. He crumbled into the water, disappearing beneath the waves like an abandoned sandcastle.

Pookiecrag stood staring at the ripples where his foe had once stood. His job was done. The thoughts, the awareness he'd had began to fade. His watery skin slowly melted into the loch from which it had come. The stones of his skeleton flew back to the island, arranging themselves – complete with moss and ivy – back where they had started.

Everything was as it was before. Except for Archie.

Even though he was covered in hugs from his friends,

he still knew that this was his responsibility. He couldn't really even blame Mrs Puddingham-Pye. She sailed into view, her smile gone but her arrogance untouched.

'Nicely played, Urchin,' she snarled. 'An inspired move, using the old family pile. A strategy so crafty it reminds me of, well, me. What kind of a person are you growing into, I wonder?' Her eyes narrowed in fury. 'I shan't forget what you've cost me tonight, boy – my road, my electricity, my factory, my world domination! One day we shall have a reckoning. And on that day, you will pay dearly.'

The sound of a distant explosion echoed across the loch.

'That'll be the twins,' giggled Garstigan. His mistress turned her gaze back towards the town, her anger subsiding.

'I really shouldn't leave them alone with dynamite,' she said lovingly. 'The banks get so annoyed when their silly safes are blown open.' And she was gone.

Audrey and the other women gathered round Archie.

'You have done well, child,' Audrey said. 'You have redeemed yourself and, furthermore, you have given us the chance to redeem ourselves. The Sisterhood of the Maelstrom has discharged its duty. The ocean is calling us. You will not see us again, not even if the Stuffed Yellowcheek is in mortal danger.'

'The Tufted Yellowbeak,' corrected Fliss.

'Whatever. It never existed anyway.'

The women waded into the black water until only their heads were visible in the moonlight. Then they too were gone, swimming to wherever they called home.

⚬

As the next day wasn't a school day, Archie knew he could have a lie-in without anyone asking awkward questions. He wrapped his quilt round him and tucked his toes underneath Sherbet's warm, soft body, as the dog snored at the end of his bed. But Archie didn't feel like sleeping, and had hardly slept all night.

The late-morning sunlight shone through a pale hand that stroked the dog's head. The ghost sat down on the edge of the bed and smiled at Archie.

'Great-Uncle Archibald!' said Archie, sitting up. 'You don't normally visit my bedroom.'

'I thought I'd see how you were doing. You've had quite a busy week, my boy.'

Archie sighed.

'It all worked out on in the end, I suppose,' he said.

'But it could have been a disaster!
It was all my fault. Mrs Puddingham-Pye was right – I
was overconfident. I made mistakes.'

'You're young, Archie. You're not just learning about
spells and magic. You're learning about *when* to use them,
where your responsibilities lie and where they don't.

'You are the Guardian of the Tree, its protector, and at
that you've been magnificent so far! But you need to

think carefully about where else you apply your powers, or you'll fall into Mrs Puddingham-Pye's trap.'

'I almost did – I wanted *The Book of the Earth* so much! I thought it would fix everything by making me a wyrdworker faster and helping me create new sweets. I pretended to myself that I was trying to help the town get a better power supply, but really I was only interested in finding the Book. I made the wrong decisions and put people in danger.'

'Wrong decisions made for the wrong reasons will lead you down a dark path. The easy way is never the best way. But wrong decisions made with a good heart are the foundation of wisdom.

'Look at your sweets. They were – I'm afraid to say – awful. However, you and your friends found uses for all of them in the end. That shows how you adapt and learn.'

Archie remembered what Mr Fairbairn had said. *Sometimes you need to have bad ideas to be able to learn to recognise a good one.*

'And it shows you've made good choices with who you have as your friends.'

'I've made some new ones too,' Archie replied, brightening. 'I hope I haven't lost Old Jings's friendship. I don't think he approved.'

Great-Uncle Archibald laughed.

'He's had to deal with many a troublesome young McBudge in his time. I wouldn't worry about that. I certainly gave him plenty of headaches in my younger days! And the Smidgenfolk are grateful for your promise to protect them. Their relatives in the mountains are dealing with all that dynamite left behind.

'Mrs Puddingham-Pye won't be getting her tunnel. And, I've heard the power company have decided not to work with her any more, after they found out what she was planning, and after their chief engineer disappeared mysteriously.'

Archie smiled. 'I spoke to them last night,' he said. 'They're going to route the cable over the mountain, without the help of magic but with the help of a donation from McBudge Confectionery Company. And via a path that keeps it far from any wildlife, thanks to Dr MacCrabbie's advice. Billy might have played a part in influencing her.'

'Good friends are good to have. Especially friends who challenge you.'

Archie nodded. 'Friends like Fliss. I should listen to her more often.'

He jumped out of bed and began pulling on his clothes.

'Feeling a bit cheerier now?' asked the ghost, who was beginning to fade into the morning light.

'Yes,' said Archie firmly. 'And I've got a busy day ahead of me.'

'Busy? But it's Saturday. There's no school.'

'I'm off to make some sweets,' said Archie. 'Really, really terrible ones. Awful ones, in fact. I can't wait to see what happens ...'

Acknowledgements

Thank you once again to Claire Powell, who has added her own magic to this book and brought Dundoodle and its inhabitants to life so vividly through her illustrations. A huge thank you to the team at Bloomsbury, particularly my patient editor Lucy Mackay-Sim, for their hard work in everything else: editing, copy-editing, design, marketing and selling! The amount of work that goes into putting a book into the world is completely mind-blowing! Lastly, thank you to the readers, reviewers, bloggers and librarians who have joined Archie and his friends on these adventures. I raise a mug of Clootie's hot chocolate in your honour!

Read about Archie's first adventure!

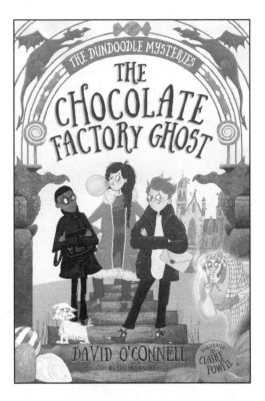

AVAILABLE NOW

Turn the page for a sneak peek!

1

Archie stared up at the portrait of the old man. It had winked at him, hadn't it? He was sure of it. No, he must be imagining things. This spooky old house was playing tricks with his mind.

He was sitting in the very grand library of the very grand Honeystone Hall, surrounded by books – how could anyone own so *many* books? – and ancient, rickety and *very* dusty furniture. Were all the cobwebs real or were they specially delivered by the We'll-Make-Your-Home-Look-Creepy Company? Mum sat in the chair next to him, fidgeting like she had spiders dancing in her underwear and too preoccupied to pay any attention to misbehaving artwork. Had the portrait winked at him again? It hadn't. Had it? It HAD! It even grinned a little. This place was seriously WEIRD.

He dragged his eyes away from the painting which hung above the very grand fireplace.

'What are we *doing* here?' he whispered for the hundredth time.

'I don't *know*,' Mum whispered back. She gave the sparrow-like man shuffling papers, who sat in front of them, a sharp look.

'Can we get on with ... *things*, Mr Tatters?' she said. 'We've come all the way from Invertinkle.'

'Of course, of course, dear lady,' said the lawyer amiably. 'Some of the details of this ... *situation* are unusual. I was just checking a few particulars, but now we can proceed.' He cleared his throat dramatically.

'Archie McBudge,' said Mr Tatters, peering at the boy through a pair of grubby spectacles. 'You are a very fortunate young man. Very fortunate *indeed*. Great things lie in store for you.'

Archie had never thought he was destined for Great Things. A few Medium-Sized Things perhaps. 'Medium-sized' always sounded manageable. Great Things sounded like a *lot* of responsibility and he wasn't the ambitious type.

'Really?' was all he could say. *What was going on?*

'Whilst we mourn the recent *tragic* loss of your

great-uncle, Archibald McBudge …' said Mr Tatters, pointing a bony finger towards the painting – *the* painting! He had a *Great-Uncle Archibald?* '… owner of McBudge's Fudge and Confectionery Company, and a dear, personal friend of mine …' Archie's jaw dropped. McBudge's Fudge! He'd never even known Great-Uncle Archibald existed, but everyone knew McBudge's Fudge. It was the softest, sweetest-tasting, melt-in-the-mouthiest, fudgiest fudge you could buy. The best in the world. Archie had always been pleased he shared his name with a company that made something so famously tasty, but he'd never thought there might be an actual family connection! And from the look on Mum's face, she hadn't either. She started to say something but was interrupted by Mr Tatters giving his beaky nose a good blow.

'Whilst we mourn his loss,' the lawyer repeated, dabbing his eyes, 'I am very pleased to tell you that your great-uncle remembered you in his will.' He picked up a leather-bound folder. Archie and Mum looked nervously at each other. Nobody had ever left them anything in a will before. They'd never known anyone with any money! All they knew was that Mr Tatters had sent them a letter asking them to drive all the way to the little town of Dundoodle, tucked between a mountain and a forest-edged loch, to meet him at Honeystone Hall to talk about some 'family business'. The lawyer was reading from a piece of paper in the folder.

'Your great-uncle writes: *As my nephew is no longer alive, I hereby leave all my earthly possessions to his son, my namesake, Archie McBudge. My fortune, my business holdings and associated properties I leave to him and his heirs.*' Mr Tatters took off his spectacles and looked at Archie expectantly.

'Oh, Archie!' said Mum with a deep intake of breath.

'What?' said Archie. He didn't understand. What were 'earthly possessions'? 'Has he left me his gardening tools or something?'

'No!' hissed Mum. 'Archie, he's left you *everything*.'

'Everything?' said Archie.

'*Everything*,' said Mr Tatters.

'Does that mean I *own* the fudge factory?' said Archie in disbelief. 'Where they make the fudge and the chocolates and all the other sweets?'

'Yes, Archie. You own the fudge factory,' confirmed Mr Tatters.

'And all the McBudge Fudge shops?' put in Mum, wide-eyed. 'There's one in almost every town.'

'And all the McBudge Fudge shops,' said Mr Tatters.

'And Honeystone Hall?' said Archie, looking around him. 'Can we come and live here? There must be over a hundred rooms in this place!' And a very odd painting, though he didn't mention that.

'*And* Honeystone Hall,' said Mr Tatters. He snapped the folder shut. 'Fudge fortune. Fudge factory. Fudge shops. Fudge … urm, *Honey*stone Hall. The whole lot. Even the gardening tools.'

I must have put my lucky underpants on today, thought Archie. He looked up at the portrait of Great-Uncle Archibald. The old man in the painting winked at him again. And this time, Archie winked back.